THE

double
life of
zoe
flynn

Also by Janet Lee Carey

Molly's Fire

Wenny Has Wings

THE double life of zoe flynn

JANET LEE CAREY

ATHENEUM BOOKS FOR YOUNG READERS
New York   London   Toronto   Sydney

To my sons, Aaron, Sean, and Joshua,
for all the moves we put you
through during your childhood years.
May each of you find a home of the heart.

And to Martha Elke,
an artist and a poet,
who was my own Aliya when
I was the new girl in town.

Atheneum Books for Young Readers
An imprint of Simon & Schuster Children's Publishing Division
1230 Avenue of the Americas
New York, New York 10020

Book design by Ann Sullivan
The text for this book is set in New Caledonia.

Manufactured in the United States of America

6 8 10 9 7 5

Library of Congress Cataloging-in-Publication Data
Carey, Janet Lee.
The double life of Zoe Flynn / Janet Lee Carey.— 1st ed.
p. cm.
Summary: When Zoe's family has to live in their van for months after moving from
California to Oregon so her father can find work, Zoe tries to keep her sixth-grade
classmates from discovering that she is homeless.
ISBN: 1-4169-6754-0   ISBN: 978-1-4169-6754-5
[1. Homeless persons—Fiction. 2. Family life—Fiction.
3. Moving, Household—Fiction.]
I. Title.
PZ7.C2125Th 2004
[Fic]—dc22   2003013777

Acknowledgments

My warmest thanks to my editors, Ginee Seo and Susan Burke, for their unwavering story analyses and clear vision of Zoe's odyssey. Thanks also to the people at the National Coalition for the Homeless (www.nationalhomeless.org) for their tireless advocacy for homeless people across the U.S., and particularly for their invaluable information on the growing population of homeless families with young children. I'm indebted to Asma Gull Hasan, author of *American Muslims: The New Generation*, and her mother, Seeme Gull Khan Hasan, who took the time to read the manuscript and to give me detailed advice regarding Aliya's family. To my son, Sean, for his courageous efforts to defend the homeless. To my friend and fellow author Indu Sundaresan for cooking me a fresh paratha in her kitchen (very good with jam!). And to author Joyce O'Keefe for inviting me to measure every square inch of Benny Lindsey's van, including the sleeping platform her father built behind the backseat. The platform was just how I'd imagined it for the book, and seeing the real thing—right down to the storage boxes underneath it— was a thrill.

1

It wasn't like an earthquake hit on that hot July day in Tillerman, but the world might as well have leaped up like a crazed bull and tried to buck Zoe off its back. If Zoe had known what was coming, she wouldn't have stuck around to help her mom with dinner. She would have gone to Kellen's house, eaten macaroni and cheese, and spent one more night as a regular kid.

Zoe thought about it later, trying to figure out the exact moment when she heard the first rumblings of her own personal earthquake. And she decided it began with hide-and-seek. Her house on 18 Hawk Road was a great place to play because it was big and old and there were tons of places to hide.

"Fifty-five. Fifty-six." Her brother, Juke, was counting in the kitchen. Kellen had already raced down the hall, but Zoe was still circling. Where to this time?

Behind the ancient piano? The storage nook under the stairs? Juke knew too many of her hiding spots, so she'd have to pull off a good disappearing act to win. She peered under the couch. Too easy.

"Seventy-eight." *Smack. Crunch.* "Seventy-nine." Juke was downing saltines while he counted. Zoe ran around the corner and made a dash for Dad's stuffed chair in the sunroom.

"Taken," whispered Kellen. She sucked on a strand of honey brown hair, and her green eyes said everything. She wasn't going to budge.

"Ninety-seven. Ninety-eight. Ninety-nine!"

Zoe flew into her parents' room, usually off-limits, but this was an emergency.

"Ready or not. Here I come!"

Zoe dove under the double bed. She was deep inside the musty dark, blowing away dust bunnies, when she saw Juke's bare feet just outside the bedroom door, his toes iced in brown dirt. He turned slowly and brushed against Grandma Nell's rocking chair. The chair rocked back and forth as if a ghost were settling in. Tension grew in her chest as Juke passed the bedroom door and headed for the dining room.

She should make a dash to the base soon, but Juke was still too close by. Better to kill a little more time under the bed. She slid on her belly just far enough to eye the photographs on the bedroom wall. Dad and Juke standing with Max outside Horizon Books before it went under. Mom with her prizewinning roses at the garden fair. Then there were those stupid baby pictures. Shots of her in a tie-dyed T-shirt and sagging diapers rocking out at a Jam for Breakfast concert. Another shot taken when she was three, sitting next to the band's drum set, eating a chocolate brownie, her round cheeks so brown, it looked like she was maybe pigging out on a hunk of mud. She'd ripped those two shots off the wall one time last year, but Dad had put them back.

Zoe licked her dry lips. What was the deal with those photos, anyway? So they captured the days when Dad took the family on tour with Jam for Breakfast. That was history. They'd put down roots here in Tillerman when she was four, and this was home now.

She listened for Juke and was considering a brave dash for home base when the phone rang. By the third ring her mom's slender feet appeared in tattered sandals and crossed the floor. "Oh, hi, honey." The bed dipped suddenly as Mom sat down, the springs catching a strand of Zoe's hair.

Zoe bit her lip and worked to untangle the brown strand as Mom talked to Dad. "Oh," said Mom, her voice low and disappointed. "Okay, Hap." There was a long pause. A sort of throaty sound. "Did you speak to Mr. Sallenger? Uh-huh. A deal already?"

Zoe listened closer. Dad had made a deal with the landlord, but then Mom didn't sound happy about it.

"No," said Mom, "it doesn't surprise me. He's been talking about that for a long time." Another low sound, like wind through a pipe. "No," said Mom. "I'm not crying. I'm not blaming you. Stop being so paranoid. Yes, I know we have to do this!" Zoe's fingers froze, mid-tangle.

"I told you I can handle it!" Mom stood up suddenly, and Zoe squealed as a hunk of hair pulled away from her scalp.

"Just a minute, Hap." A pale face with long black hair appeared under the bed. "Zoe, get out from under there. Now!"

Zoe's T-shirt gathered dust as she scooted out from under the bed. "Hide-and-seek," whispered Zoe, but Mom looked stern, as if Zoe had been purposefully spying on her.

"It's nothing, Hap," said Mom as Zoe fled the room. "Just a game the kids are playing."

Zoe's legs felt heavy as she started for home base in the kitchen. She didn't care so much about being caught now. She wanted to be caught. She stood in the living room feeling the white heat zap through the front window. It fell across her bare feet and lit up the red-gold pattern in the Persian carpet.

Merlin trotted up the stairs and licked her hand. She rubbed his soft golden fur.

"Hey!" shouted Juke as he rounded the corner. "One two three on Zoe!"

"Yeah, sure," said Zoe. "You got me." She tipped her head, trying to hear more of the conversation in the next room. Was Mom crying? Juke shrugged and ran off to find Kellen, and the room was quiet again.

Outside in the front yard the trees were still, not even a whisper of wind in the branches. Then there was a familiar rattling sound as the old pipes under the floorboards pumped water to the master bathroom. The toilet flushed, gurgled, and Mom raced out of her bedroom. "Zoe? Run and get the plunger, quick. The toilet's stopped up again!"

Ten minutes later Mom was still cursing and plunging the toilet. Kellen was on her way home, and Zoe was told to set the table.

Game over.

It was the last game Zoe ever played at 18 Hawk Road.

Steam rose from the soup pot, filling the air with the odor of cooked onions. It was too hot for soup, but food had been scarce since Horizon Books went under and onions were cheap. Plates and bowls were already on the table. Zoe slid open a drawer and pulled out four spoons. Mom came in, paused, and blew upward, her bangs fluttering like startled blackbirds.

"Toilet okay?" asked Zoe.

"Doesn't matter," said Mom.

"What do you mean?"

Mom didn't answer. That wasn't like Mom, but then, she'd been pretty uptight ever since Dad lost his teaching job and the bookstore, too. Zoe grabbed the napkins and left her in the kitchen, leaning over the counter, tossing the lettuce and tomatoes fiercely, as if they were in the way of something she wanted at the bottom of the bowl.

Half an hour later the family gathered for dinner. Dad set the soup pot on the hot pad and took his seat at the head of the table. Onion soup and corn bread in July. Heat on heat. The soup steamed. The corn bread bent the air above the pan like a mirage. The damp air glued Dad's gray-blond hair to his forehead. He pulled it back and adjusted his ponytail before opening his napkin.

Mom's lip quivered as Dad served the soup. No one mentioned today's job interview, even though the *no* hung over all of them and wrung sweat from their skin like the soup steam. Zoe stared out the cracked old window to the backyard. Twilight. The acacia branches moved slowly in the wind, as if they were under water. The tree looked cool and inviting. She decided to eat fast, run outside, leap onto the tire swing, and fly over the ravine. She'd swing till the moon and stars came out. All she had to do was finish her soup and corn bread.

After dinner Dad passed around a plate of Oreos for dessert. A real treat like they hadn't seen in months. Zoe wanted to say *What gives?* but then she lost her mouth to the crisp chocolate and sweet cream filling. She was dunking her second cookie when Dad leaned back in his chair and said he didn't get the job. No surprise there.

Juke licked the creamy center of his Oreo and told Dad to find another job in town.

"The trouble is, we're living in such a small town. And with the economy the way it is . . ." Dad crossed his arms. "I've tried for months now. I've looked in Tillerman and hunted for work a couple of hours' drive in all directions. Too many places going out of business around here. There just aren't any job openings."

Mom cleared her throat and toyed with her water glass. Dad leaned forward. "Mom and I have talked it over. We've tried everything, and it's just not . . . it's time to move on and look for work elsewhere."

"Move on?" whispered Zoe.

"To where, Dad?" asked Juke.

"We'll head north," said Mom, trying to smile. She reached for Dad's hand. "Some of the college towns up there will probably have work."

"It'll be an adventure," said Dad.

"Like the years you toured with Jam for Breakfast?" said Juke.

"Not exactly," said Dad.

"No," said Zoe.

Dad leaned back in his chair. "It's not like we have much choice, honey."

"What about Merlin?"

"Max and June said they'll keep Merlin for us until we find a place to—"

"You guys go ahead," said Zoe. "I'll stay here."

"Honey, you can't stay. We have to be out by the end of the week. Mr. Sallenger's got a buyer."

Zoe leaped up. "18 Hawk Road? For sale? When did he do that?"

"He's had an interested family ready to buy for a

while now, and it looks like the deal's going to go through."

So this was "the deal" with Mr. Sallenger that Mom had mentioned in the phone call. "But he can't kick us out! This is our home! "

"Zoe, we can't go on living here," said Dad. "I know you're upset, but we have to move on."

Zoe steadied herself against the chair. The rumblings she'd felt earlier had accelerated, and the quake was definitely hitting her now. "Who'd want to buy this old place?" she yelled. "With stains on the wood floors, leaky pipes, the furnace that conks out every winter, the backed-up toilets that have to be flushed three times, the—"

"Zoe, sit down," said Dad, pressing his index finger on the table. But Zoe turned and raced from the dining room with Merlin at her heels. Downstairs she closed her bedroom door and turned the lock.

Her heart splashed down like some stupid stone in some stupid river. She went cold all over. This was her house. The whole crazy, crooked place. The sunroom with its sloping floors you could roll your marbles down. The wide, bright living room. The walls with sagging wallpaper. The sinks that coughed and spat when you turned them on. She knew every creak and crack and cranky sound of the place.

Merlin wagged his tail and licked her bare feet. "Cut it out, Mer." She stepped into the center of her room, feeling the cool linoleum floor on the soles of her feet.

She'd stay here. They couldn't make her move. Not if the door was locked.

Outside the sky was turning deep blue. Her toys and stacks of games turned into blue shadows as the room filled with twilight. Even the glass knob on her closet door was blue, as if a secret ocean were slowly flooding her room.

From the hall behind her came the sound of footsteps. Dad knocked on her door. "Zoe? Can I come in?"

"No."

"Zoe, don't do this."

Zoe stood still until the knocking stopped. The air was thick with color. Zoe moved her arms. Swimming in it. Losing herself in the middle of the blue.

2

Rapunzel was rescued from her tower by a prince climbing up her long hair. Sleeping Beauty's prince battled through one hundred years of thorns, passing other suitors' skeletons along the way. Zoe's dad gave up knocking at her door, went outside, and leaned against her windowsill.

Framed in the open window, his long hair lit up in the moonlight. The soft glow erased the wrinkles around his eyes and mouth. He looked like a surfer who'd lost his way home from the beach. "Hello," he said.

Merlin bounced over and put his paws on the sill. His tail brushed against Zoe's leg as she stepped closer. She peered out the window like a dark-haired Rapunzel who'd blown her chance of rescue on a cute haircut. "Okay, hello," she said.

Dad reached up and brushed back Zoe's bangs. "Don't be mad, Zoe."

"I don't want to go."

"I don't either, honey."

Zoe scanned her dad's blue eyes. He'd always wanted to get back on the road, hadn't he?

"There's no work for me here in Tillerman. And none any driving distance from here. You know I've tried."

She did know how hard he'd looked. Still, she had to ask: "What about the college?"

"I wasn't the only faculty member to be laid off last year. I'm afraid they're still in a slump over there."

"The library?"

"Tried that."

"Tillerman Hardware?"

"It's closing down next month."

Zoe's eyes opened wide. "What will Mr. Yamamoto do?"

"I don't know, honey. Maybe he'll have to move to another town, like us."

Zoe didn't mention the one McDonald's in town. Vegetarians weren't into flipping burgers for a living.

"Dizzie's Thrift?"

"Minimum wage." He ran his fingers through his hair. "Combined with Mom's housecleaning money, we still wouldn't earn enough for rent. Even if we could, Mr. Sallenger's not willing to offer a new lease now that he's got a buyer."

Zoe leaned on her elbows. There had to be a way. "If only Horizon Books hadn't gone under," she said.

Dad nodded. "It was a great bookstore, wasn't it? I miss it almost every day."

Okay, he missed the store, but that would be nothing compared to how she'd feel if they left this house. She had to tell Dad that. She had to make him understand. Somehow her room had always been the center of the universe, and everything else had spun around it. She knew the universe didn't really work that way. Still, for her, this particular spot on planet Earth was her center of gravity. It was the first place she'd ever called home after touring with Dad's band when she was small, and she'd loved it from the moment she'd stepped inside. It was her very own bedroom. A place where she could be Zoe alone.

"Penny for your thoughts," said Dad.

"You got one?"

Dad fished in his jeans pocket, pulled out a dime, and placed it on the sill.

"I don't remember much about living on the road," said Zoe.

"We had some fun back then."

"It's not about rock-'n'- roll this time, Dad." She saw him flinch, and her mouth went dry.

Zoe held the dime to the glass. She thought about their days on the road before they'd settled here in town. She'd been three years old then, and the memories were a kaleidoscope of colors, songs, and smells. Sometimes she'd gotten a whiff of her past when Dad pumped gas down at the station. The strange familiar smell of good-bye.

"I made pretty good money managing the band," said

Dad. "Enough to finish my Ph.D., get us settled here in Tillerman, and go in on the bookstore venture."

"Yeah," said Zoe, "I know."

The man in the moon poured quicksilver over the trees. Zoe pressed her chin into her palms. What good was a Ph.D. in English literature when you couldn't make the rent? She had to come up with something for Dad. She couldn't leave Kellen to face sixth grade at Creekside School alone this year. Besides, she had plans. She and Kellen had finally figured out a way to get revenge on Chris Tucker. A beautiful plan involving a series of love notes soaked in disgusting perfume and jammed in Chris's locker every day until he cracked.

"What about your fantasy book?" asked Zoe.

"I still haven't sold *The Dragons of Morenth* yet."

"Cool title."

"Thanks." Dad leaned against the wall. "You coming out?"

"Nope."

"Okay," said Dad. "Are you going to be all right?"

"I need to think."

"Well, if you need to talk some more . . ." He leaned in a little closer; his daylight blue eyes were all that was left of the day now that night was at his back. Dad smiled once, then disappeared around the side of the house, his feet making crunching noises in the gravel.

"Come on, Merlin." Zoe grabbed the glass doorknob and ducked into her closet dreamroom. She wiggled down into her beanbag chair. Merlin curled up at her feet as she shut the door and flicked on the flashlight.

If only she could find a door into another world the way characters in books did. This would be a good time to leave the real world behind, with everything falling apart the way it was. She wouldn't mind fighting the White Witch in Narnia, having tea with the Mad Hatter in Wonderland, or dancing with the Scarecrow in Oz. Maybe if she found the magic door into a new world and slipped away for a while, everything would be different when she returned. Dad would have found a job while she was gone, and they wouldn't have to leave Tillerman.

Zoe grabbed *The Wonderful Wizard of Oz* from her closet bookshelf and began reading it again for the fourth time. On page five it said, "The north and south winds met where the house stood, and made it the exact center of the cyclone." In her mind she saw Dorothy's house spinning higher and higher up into the sky. She waited for the picture to take shape behind her eyes, then grabbed her drawing pad and turned to a fresh page. She drew the cyclone spiraling up the paper in blue and gray and black, and on top of that she added Dorothy's house. She sketched in the pale yellow flashlight, humming as she pushed against the oil chalk till the drawing was complete.

Okay, Dorothy had been sucked up into Oz, but she *wanted* to leave Kansas. And she got to take her house with her. Her house *and* her dog.

Merlin panted, his breath as rank as a gym locker.

Zoe kissed his ear anyway and jammed her bare feet under his soft belly. "I won't leave you, stinky boy. I promise." She held the flashlight above his head and circled it round and round till the shirts and the dresses and the empty hangers spun in her own silent tornado.

3

Zoe staggered up the garden steps with a box of toys and placed it in the detached garage beside Mom's old exercise bike. Last night she and Juke were told to fill a backpack and book bag with clothes and "special things" they'd be taking on the road. The rest of the stuff would be stored in Max and June's basement or sold at the garage sale.

Dad came in, kissed Mom on the cheek, and put another box of books on the floor. "They're all priced," he said before turning to Zoe. "Honey, can you give me a hand upstairs?"

Zoe followed him up the steps on the back side of the garage and entered his dusty office. Computer gone, desk gone, shelves gone, posters rolled up into white tubes, the room looked like a storage room above the garage instead of a cozy writer's office. Dust motes swirled in the dim sunlight. Zoe fought off a sneeze as

Dad filled another box, placing the books carefully inside as if they were eggs.

Two boxes left and one book on the floor. Zoe picked up *The Hobbit*.

"It's for you," said Dad. "A journey tale. The best kind of book to take on a quest."

"What's our quest?" asked Zoe.

"Find a job. Another place to live."

"So it's not about living on the road, like when I was three?"

Dad wiped off his hands and flipped over the lid. "Only until I get work."

Zoe looked out the dusty window at her house below. "Couldn't we stay somewhere else in town?"

Dad put his arm around her. "Where?"

Zoe thought about it. If this had happened a year ago, they could have moved in with Grandma Nell, but she was in a nursing home now.

"Even if we had a place to stay around here," said Dad, as if completing her thought, "we'd still have the problem of finding work." Dad gave her shoulder a squeeze, then handed her a box and nodded toward the door.

She was downstairs pricing dishes with Mom when the first car pulled up. Jamie Martin, with blond pigtails and rumpled clothes, led her two-hundred-pound mom into the garage.

"I've got stuff to do down in the house," said Zoe, and she beat it out of there fast. Down in the living room Zoe ran her finger along the empty bookshelves. The coffee table had a price tag on it. So did the couch. She lay belly down on the old Persian carpet. Okay, she'd have to mellow out or she'd never make it through the day. Her finger traced the magical mountainsides hidden in the red-gold design on the rug. Each mountain peak was covered in golden snow. The dry, sweet smell of chamomile clung to the carpet where she'd spilled a cup of tea there last winter. She lay her cheek against the scratchy wool and breathed in the scent.

"Lots of furniture in here!" Dad said, bursting through the kitchen door. Zoe bolted for the stairway.

"Nice dining-room table," said a woman's voice. Zoe ran downstairs, slid into her room, and slammed her bedroom door.

She gulped for air, trying to calm herself, but the sound of footsteps coming down the stairs got her heart pounding even faster.

"It's a good solid bed," she heard Dad saying. "Maple frame. Old-fashioned bedposts."

Zoe dove into her closet, wedged herself tight in her beanbag chair, and peeked through the crack as Dad came in with Jamie Martin's mom.

"Jamie's shooting up," said Mrs. Martin, running her freckled hand along a bedpost. "What do you think, honey?"

Jamie skipped across the room and traced the dark hole in the poppy wallpaper. Her pigtails bounced as she leaped onto the bed and crossed her legs. "I guess so," she said before blowing an enormous pink bubble.

Pop! And that was that. Mrs. Martin was scrawling out a check for Dad, her checkbook pressed against the bedpost. Jamie fell backward and lay straight as a rolling pin atop Zoe's pillows. She rolled from side to side, the star quilt Grandma Nell made flattening under Jamie's weight like cookie dough.

"Come on, honey," said her mom. "We'll pick the bed up later. We'll get Papa to bring the truck."

Jamie spread her arms wide, moving them back and forth as if she were making angels in the snow. She stared at the ceiling, her eyes growing wide as she blew a triumphant bubble. *Pop!* The bed was hers.

That night Zoe held her pillow tight against her chest. Bed gone, shelves gone, games sold or packed. She curled inside her sleeping bag, letting the coolness of the old brown floor soak into her back. Moonlight fell through the window, poured through her glass knob, and sharpened into a white arrow across her floor. She ran her hand along the tip of light and looked at the hole in her poppy wallpaper, a secret rabbit hole in a wild garden. She turned onto her back and stared at the crack on the ceiling, an almost-elephant with an extra-long trunk. She'd pointed him out to Dad one night when she was four, and Dad said, "He'll watch over you because elephants never forget." And she'd let him guard her through good dreams, bad dreams, days alone making cardboard castles, and long afternoons spent in bed with a fever.

The glass doorknob, her closet dreamroom, the hole in the wall, the almost-elephant—they would stay in her room always, but tomorrow she would be gone. Zoe's fingertips tingled. If only she could shrink her room down to the size of a matchbox and slip it in her pocket. Come to think of it, if she had the power to do that, she'd shrink it all down. Her house, Kellen's, Dizzie's Thrift, Horizon Books (the way it looked before it closed), Creekside School, Fletcher Park, where she'd first learned to ride her bike, Yarrow Creek. The whole town of Tillerman. She'd shrink it all down, put it in her pocket, and take it with her on the road. Everything would be small and secret, and she'd protect Tillerman always.

In the center of her floor, in the center of her room, in the center of her house, in the center of the world, Zoe closed her eyes, shrinking first her house, then Kellen's, and slowly, very slowly, the whole town.

4

Up in the tree house Zoe carved her name in the acacia branch. She was just slipping her Swiss army knife back in her pocket when Kellen climbed up with some Popsicles to share. They spent their last hour together high above the rest of the world. It was hard to talk. Pretty soon the Flynns would be leaving Tillerman, not just for a week or a month or a year—but for good.

Zoe finished her orange Popsicle and sucked on the stick. Her lips still felt numb as she curled her tongue around the wood. Kellen turned and gave her an orange smile. "Saw the people who are buying your house. Skinny girl in a dumb pink lace top."

"She's a city kid named Jessica Jacobs," said Zoe. "She's supposedly got a kid sister, Mindy or Mandy or something, but I didn't meet her. Anyway, Dad made me shake Jessica's hand before she and her mom toured the house with Mr. Sallenger. Jessica checked out my bathroom and saw the pan at the base of the toilet—you know, the one that's there to catch the drip?"

"Yeah."

"She told her mom it was disgusting."

Kellen swung her legs through the tree house railings, her toenail polish glinting in the sun. "Why? It's just water."

Zoe leaned against the acacia trunk. "I know. Merlin drinks out of my toilet all the time. It's like, duh, what does the kid want?"

"Servants," quipped Kellen, tossing back her hair.

"A personal maid standing at full attention in her bathroom with a toilet brush over her shoulder, ready to scrub up every time she takes a pee."

Kellen arched her neck. "There's a spot of toothpaste on my sink! Remove it, please."

"Jessica wouldn't say 'please,'" corrected Zoe. "She'd just point and say, 'Get rid of it'!"

Kellen pointed across the yard to the trash can against the back wall of Zoe's house. "Disgusting. Get rid of it!"

Zoe pointed through the trees to Kellen's old swing set near her back deck. "Get rid of it!"

Kellen laughed, nodding toward her sister's sandbox. "Get rid of it."

Zoe flung her hand in the direction of their old green van. "Get rid of it!"

"Yeah," said Kellen. "Get rid of it forever!"

Silence.

Zoe snapped her Popsicle stick in half. The van was packed and ready to go. Sleeping bags, clothes, camping stuff. The bicycles tied to the bike rack at the rear of the van. Pretty soon it would be gone forever. It would disappear down Hawk Road with Zoe inside.

"I'll never make friends with Jessica," said Kellen.

"Never?"

"Not in a million years."

"Promise?"

"Promise." Kellen eyed the paper sack Zoe had hidden in the branch. "What's in there?"

"Guess," said Zoe, pulling it down and handing it to Kellen.

Kellen's green eyes narrowed with concentration as she felt the contours of the sack. "Not a radio."

"You wish."

"Or a cell phone."

"Yeah, right."

"Mom says they're good in emergencies."

"Yeah, emergencies like calls from Matt Kinsey."

Kellen rolled her eyes. "Right, like he'd call me!" She reached into the sack and pulled out a porcelain horse.

"I saved it from the garage sale box. I know how much you've wanted Black Beauty."

"Since I was about eight." Kellen's face was at full grin.

In third grade they'd gone to Horizon Books once a week to hear Zoe's dad read *Black Beauty*. A small group of girls, all of them mad about horses. Zoe had won the porcelain horse in a drawing on the last day.

A rush of warm wind blew Kellen's honey-colored hair across her cheek. "You shouldn't give him to me, Zoe, he's—"

"Yours," insisted Zoe. "Put him on your bedside shelf next to your glass ship. That way he'll have a home."

"I don't want you to go," said Kellen suddenly. "We've been together since preschool. What will I . . . I can't do sixth grade alone."

"You'll be all right."

"No, I won't."

"Yes, you will."

Dad came outside. "Zoe? Time to hit the road!"

Zoe started climbing down the tree. "You can sponge Black Beauty off with soapy water if he gets dusty." She gripped a thick branch and lowered her foot down to the branch below. "And don't let Meg handle him; she'd probably break him."

"I won't."

Zoe jumped to the ground with a thud. In the tree above, Kellen inched her way along the branch.

"Don't come down yet," said Zoe, brushing her hands on her shorts. "I want you to wave to me from the tree."

"Send a postcard."

"Sure."

"I mean, really send me one."

"I will."

"And if you can score a computer and get an e-mail account—"

"Yeah, instant messaging. I know."

Zoe shoved the tire swing out over the ravine, watching it spin empty in the air. Slowly, she turned her back on Kellen, on the tree, the swing, all the summers spent doing nothing in the blowing branches. Then she walked up the path past her house, touching the cracked white paint with her fingers as she passed beneath her bedroom window.

Zoe gripped the sill, pulled herself up, and peered inside her bedroom. It looked as hot and hollow as her throat.

"Zoe?" called Mom from the street above. "Zoe? Where are you? It's time to go!"

She stared at the glass doorknob Grandma Nell had given her on her seventh birthday. After the party Grandma had helped her replace the old closet doorknob with the glass one. They'd stood back to admire the way the sunlight whispered rainbows through the glass. The knob was doing that now, catching light, tossing rainbows on her bare wall. She looked at her closet door, entrance to her dreamroom. The place she'd gone to read, to draw.

Her bedroom was empty now. But her dreamroom was still there. It would always be there.

"Zoe!" called Dad, coming around the back of the house. She lowered herself down from the sill.

"There you are. You know we've gotta get going now."

"I'm—I'm—," stuttered Zoe.

"What is it, honey?"

"I've gotta go."

"What, now? The house is all locked up. Can't you wait till we get to—"

"No! I've gotta go now."

"All right." They trailed up the hill past the garden and Dad unlocked the kitchen door. "Hurry up, Zoe," he said. "And don't make a mess. We're depending on getting back our cleaning deposit."

"Don't worry," called Zoe as she crossed the kitchen. Racing downstairs, Zoe used the bathroom, flushed the toilet, rinsed her hands, dried them on her shorts, and headed for her closet.

In a few days Jessica would move in, hang her sweatshirts on the hooks, toss her sneakers on the floor, and pile Zoe's dreamroom full of dirty laundry. She didn't have much time. Pulling out her Swiss army knife, she flicked out the screwdriver and pressed it into the base of the doorknob. The glass knob was the only way in. Without it, nobody would be able to find her dreamroom. Nobody.

A few minutes later Zoe raced upstairs and burst through the kitchen door.

"You feeling all right, honey?" asked Dad.

"Yeah, Dad."

"It's just, well, you took so long, I was wondering if you were feeling—"

"My stomach hurts a little." She took her dad's hand.

"Come on," she said, leading him outside. There was no way she was going to chance him going downstairs and discovering what she'd done to her closet door.

Dad locked the kitchen door. Zoe said good-bye to the cherry tree as they climbed the garden path to the street. Strapped into the backseat of the Chevy van between Juke and Merlin, she spotted Kellen waving to her from the tree house.

As they were pulling away Zoe opened the window and stuck her head out. Everything she wanted to say to Kellen came out in a sudden jumble, like word litter. "Don't be afraid of Rita Singer! She hasn't got the guts to punch you out like she said she would. Kiss the acacia once a day for me. Remember to pour gardenia perfume on the letter and jam it in Chris's locker on the first day of school. Don't let the new girl ruin my room! Don't change! Don't ever change!"

She was still shouting this as the van swept around the corner and headed downhill.

5

Max and June Volger lived about an
hour from Tillerman in Calloway. It was close to ninety
degrees out when they pulled into the driveway, but
inside the living room was cool and dark. The whole
house smelled like french fries, sausages, and cigars. Zoe
tapped on the fishbowl and searched the murky water for
any signs of Fred and Barney, the goldfish, while Mom
went over the list with Max.

"Merlin will try to get more food out of you, but stick
to two small bowls a day," said Mom. Max dipped a handful of french fries in ketchup. "Got it," he said, jamming
the fries in his mouth.

"We usually brush him once a week," continued
Mom.

"Sure, no problem, Sadie," said Max.

A breeze played with the living-room curtains.
Outside the window, June was pulling up handfuls of

weeds and tossing them into the wheelbarrow. Max had lost Horizon Books right along with Dad. But June made pretty good money teaching second grade, so they were staying put here in Calloway.

Juke ran past the window and tossed Merlin a Frisbee. Merlin leaped up and caught it like a pro.

"Good boy!" shouted Juke. He raced up, gave Merlin a hug, then turned and tossed the Frisbee to Dad.

Zoe went out to the front lawn. "Here, boy!" she called. Merlin bounced up to her, his reddish gold fur glistening in the sunshine.

Zoe knelt down and scratched Merlin behind his ears. "You think we're just here to play, don't you, boy?" Merlin thumped his tail on the grass. "I know I promised I wouldn't leave you," said Zoe. "But it won't be forever. I swear. As soon as we get a house, we'll come back for you, Mer." Merlin looked away, distracted by the flying Frisbee.

Zoe grabbed his furry head and turned his face toward her. "Pay attention, boy! This is important! We're leaving you here for a while." Merlin panted happily. "Maybe for a long time and . . . I don't want you to forget me. I don't want you to ever—"

Merlin licked the tears off her cheek.

"Stop it, Mer!" Zoe threw her arms around him. "I love you, you stupid dog! You stupid, stupid dog."

That night they cooked their tofu hot dogs over the beach fire. Zoe and Juke made marshmallow animals on sticks and roasted them alive over the flames. And, hey, it was really fun as long as Zoe pretended they were camping, only camping, and that they'd be heading home in a few days. Dad pulled out his guitar and starting singing his favorite Jam for Breakfast songs. Zoe set her marshmallow horse on fire as Dad sang, "She left me with a song like some bird flyin'."

Zoe lifted her flaming horse to the night, like Pegasus on fire. In her mind she rode the horse across the heavens, and the wind in her face smelled like the sea.

Now Mom and Dad were singing, "Left me singin' out under the stars."

Zoe blew out the flames and tasted the charred horse.

If stars had any taste, they'd taste like that.

They'd taste just like that.

6

On the second night a summer storm blew up the coast, so instead of the nice, big tent, they were all crammed inside the van. Dad turned around and peered at Juke and Zoe. "We'll flip for who gets to sleep on the backseat," he said. "Heads or tails?"

"Tails," said Juke.

Dad flipped the quarter.

"Heads, you lose," said Zoe.

"No fair!" said Juke. "Flip it again."

"You said tails, Juke," reminded Mom.

"Yeah, well, I meant heads!"

"I'll sweep off the floor, honey, and we have a puffy mat."

"Zoe can have the puffy mat!"

Zoe crossed her arms. "I've got the seat!"

"Kids," said Dad, "it's just a summer storm and it'll pass. The next time it rains, Zoe will let Juke have the seat. Right, Zoe?" Dad was giving her the "be a good big sister" look.

"Sure," said Zoe. It was July, after all. How often was it going to rain like this?

Mom swept the floor in front of the backseat and rolled out the puffy mat. The floor space was just wide enough and long enough for a kid to nestle down in. Not too much different from the backseat, except that it was down below. Behind the backseat Dad laid out two sleeping bags on the built-in wood platform he'd made years ago. Dad wasn't exactly "Mr. Tool Guy," but he was proud of that platform. During the day most of their supplies could be stashed under the platform. At night it made a pretty good double bed with its thin foam mattress on top.

Dad flicked off the flashlight. "Who wants a movie of the mind?"

"I do," said Zoe.

"Me too," said Juke.

"Okay, close your eyes and get your screens ready. Are your eyes closed?"

"Yep," both Zoe and Juke said at once.

"Picture a pirate ship," said Dad. As the rain tapped against the van windows Dad told the story of Barnacle Jack the pirate until Juke was snoring softly on the floor below.

Zoe wished she could fall asleep that easily. She rolled over and scrunched down in her bag. The seat felt hard against her spine. She changed positions, trying not to think of the softness of her bed in her old room, the feeling that her toys were guarding her, the mixed aromas of clay and crayons, and the faint smell of chocolate that used to emanate from the crumpled candy wrappers. She tried not to think about how heavy her feet used to feel under Merlin's weight as he curled up on her bed. He was probably snoozing at the foot of Max and June's bed right now. Their feet were probably warmer than they'd felt in years.

In the middle of the night she awoke and listened. The rain had ceased, but somewhere outside, an owl hooted in the trees. The night spoke in layers of sound, behind the owl's call she could hear the wind singing in the trees and, behind that, waves pounding the shore. Zoe sat up and pushed back the curtain. The cypress trees looked blue black against the starry sky. Giant trees spreading out their arms, one tree touching the moon.

If she had her chalks with her, she'd choose a black one and a blue one to color the trees, and she'd color the moon creamy white, just the way it looked right now behind the clouds. But her chalks were packed away, and she couldn't draw here anyway. She had to be alone to draw things the way she saw them. She hadn't been able to let anyone see her artwork since the pink moon incident in first grade.

Zoe flipped onto her side and curled her toes. She could still remember the sound of the whole class laughing as Ms. Snell held up her painting and grilled her. "What color is the moon, Zoe?"

"White," said Zoe. She added the word "usually" so quietly that no one else could hear, because sometimes the moon wore a pink shade at sunset.

"And what color are trees?"

Zoe had sucked her lip. She knew the answer Ms. Snell wanted, but she didn't want to give it to her because bark wasn't always brown; sometimes it was white or gray. And leaves weren't only green; sometimes they were cream-colored underneath, and some trees had blue needles. And, anyway, she'd painted the redwoods in her picture blue because it was twilight, and all the redwoods by her house turned blue that time of day. But she couldn't tell Ms. Snell that.

Meanwhile, kids' hands shot up all around her. Everyone was saying, "Oh! I know. I know." And Christopher had shouted "Trees are green!" because he couldn't hold it in any longer, and Ms. Snell offered him a smile. It had happened a long time ago now, but her gut still tightened whenever she thought about it.

A bird swooped by. Probably the owl. She tried not to think about the stuff that had happened at Creekside School. Ms. Snell had left the next year, and most of her memories of Creekside after that were good ones. It didn't matter what she thought about Creekside now, anyway, because she wouldn't be going back there again.

7

At two o'clock the next afternoon they pulled into the parking lot of Rolling Hills Rest Home and entered the big, square building. Zoe had been excited about the visit. She hadn't seen Grandma Nell in such a long time, but now that they were here, she was feeling nervous.

"Stinks," said Juke, pinching his nose.

Like a toilet bowl, thought Zoe.

"Juke," warned Mom, "stop pinching your nose!"

"I gotta," said Juke. "I'll barf."

Mom pulled his hand away. "I mean it, Juke."

Zoe's sneakers squeaked against the bare floor as she and Juke followed Mom and Dad down the long white hall. "Why'd Grandma Nell have to come here?" said Juke, catching up to Mom. "She used to have a nice house, and this place stinks."

"Quiet, Juke! Not another word."

The nurse pushed open the door. "Nell," she said in a loud voice, "you have visitors."

Zoe crept by an old woman in a wheelchair who was clicking her tongue in rhythm to the toilet paper ad on TV. She skirted the bed curtain to see her dad leaning over Grandma's hospital bed. "Mom?" he said, touching her hand.

"Sean?" said Grandma.

"No, Mom, it's me, Hap, and Sadie's here too, with the kids."

"Sean, where were you?" scolded Grandma. "You missed dinner!"

Dad gave Grandma Nell a kiss, even though she thought the kiss was coming from Grandpa Flynn who died three years ago.

"I've made applesauce, Sean," said Grandma.

"Mom, it's me, Hap," said Dad again.

Zoe stared at the TV. A blue-eyed girl was jumping through a hula hoop, and the clouds were raining rainbow-colored candies. She wanted to jump inside the TV right now and run through the candy rain. The real world was creeping her out. Dad had warned her that Grandma's Alzheimer's had gotten worse. But she never thought it would be this bad. Okay, Grandma had forgotten stuff the last time they'd visited her house. She couldn't remember where she'd put her sweater, and she kept saying the same thing over and over, like each time was the first time, but she'd remembered her own son, for gosh sakes!

Zoe jammed her hand in her overalls pocket and grabbed her glass doorknob. The little girl on TV was catching handfuls of red and yellow candy. Like everything was just that sweet and easy. It made Zoe's belly ache.

"Zoe?" said Mom. "Juke? Come on over and talk to Grandma."

Juke tugged on the yellow curtain that separated the beds. "I've gotta use the can," he said.

"Come on, kids," said Dad. Mom stepped around the bed and gave Juke a kiss on the cheek. "Just say hello," she whispered. Juke shot Zoe a "you first" look.

"Forget it," whispered Zoe.

"We've had to leave Tillerman," Dad was saying. "But once I've landed a job and we're settled down again, we'll come back by to visit with you, Mom."

Grandma's head was moving back and forth like she was viewing a tennis match. A tuft of gray hair stuck out above her left ear.

"Juke and Zoe are here to see you, Mom," said Dad.

Juke stepped up to Grandma's bed and pushed one of the buttons on the rail. Grandma's bed sang a high-pitched tune, like a chorus of dolphins, as it began to rise.

"Ohhh!" said Grandma Nell, her eyes wide with delight.

"Cut it out, Juke," warned Mom. Now Grandma was above them, as high in the air as the girl in *The Princess and the Pea,* only she wasn't a girl and there wasn't any prince and the only peas served up at Rolling Hills were probably whirled in the institutional blender.

Grandma looked down and shook her head at Juke. "Don't open it," she said. "Wait until your father comes home."

"Open what?" asked Juke.

"Don't sass me, child!" scolded Grandma, her blue eyes suddenly icy as she peered over the side of her bed.

Dad pushed another button, and Grandma slowly descended. Zoe held her breath. It was her turn next. If she didn't get out of this room quick, she was gonna pee her pants—not that anyone at Rolling Hills would notice.

"Hey, Grandma Nell," said Zoe. "It's me, Zoe." Stupid of her. Dad had tried the same line, and Grandma had thought he was Grandpa Flynn.

"Zoe," repeated Grandma.

Zoe nearly jumped out of her skin. "Yeah, it's me," she said, sliding her sweaty fingers across the glass knob in her pocket.

Grandma lifted her brown freckled hand and tucked Zoe's hair behind her ear. "Zoe," she said again.

"Yes, Grandma?"

Grandma licked her dry lips. Her head began to sway. "Find the door," she said.

8

It was a gray August morning. A damp skirt of fog surrounded the van. At the edge of the campsite Dad perched on a log with a towel draped over his shoulders. "Are you ready?" he asked.

"Just a sec," said Mom. "I'm looking for the scissors."

Zoe crossed her arms and leaned against the van. All her life Dad's long hair had been pulled back in a ponytail, and it had never gotten in the way of finding a job before. But things were changing and jobs were tighter.

"Here they are," said Mom.

Zoe left Dad on the log waiting for his haircut. She wasn't sure she wanted to hang around and watch the transformation.

Sea oats brushed against her legs as she walked down to the beach.

Almost two months of camping out while Dad looked for work. Town to town, he'd checked the Internet job lines and scanned the Help Wanted section in the papers. Most of the time the jobs were filled by the time Dad made the phone call or drove up in the van. And whenever he scored an interview, it always came up dry. What he really needed was a teaching job, but they were scarce.

Down at the shore Zoe heard the pounding waves with her whole body, feeling each one like a watery smack-down heartbeat. Storm clouds approached, as heavy and hunchbacked as a herd of buffalo. She closed her eyes and smelled the salty air. Dad had another interview lined up this afternoon, and today they were crossing the border into Oregon. She didn't like the idea of leaving California, but then, he'd had lots of interviews and this one probably wouldn't amount to anything. Behind her eyelids she could see Dad's hair falling onto the sandy ground. Zoe shook her head and opened her eyes again just in time to see the rain coming across the water in great gray curtains.

Feet rooted in the sand, she let the wall of water hit her. The rush of it like wet fingers—the feel of Grandma Nell's hands when she used to scrub her hair. Another gust of wind brought her last words to shore. *Find the door.*

Grandma Nell was pretty sick with Alzheimer's now. Still, those three words continued to echo inside Zoe's head. She'd been looking for the door into another world all her life. Lucy had found her way to Narnia by opening a wardrobe door. Alice had found the door to another world by falling down a rabbit hole and, later, by sliding through a looking glass.

How was she supposed to find the magic door when the only doors she'd opened lately were attached to campground lavatories, gas station rest rooms, and the public library where Dad had spent hours on the Internet? Maybe she should face the fact that Grandma's deck was missing more than a few cards. Everyone else had.

Then again, maybe Grandma Nell was talking about finding another secret place, like the closet in her bedroom. Grandma Nell was the one who gave her the glass doorknob in the first place. She'd understood Zoe's need to find a place to draw alone after the embarrassing pink moon incident. And she'd helped Zoe screw it into her closet door, so Grandma knew about her dreamroom before anyone else in her family had. Zoe wiped her wet bangs away from her eyes. It had been almost two months since she'd been alone for long enough to draw. Maybe when they found a new house, she'd have her own closet again.

She tasted the rain on her lips. The storm had come across the sea to meet her. From somewhere far behind, she could hear Mom calling, "Zoe! Come on!"

A few minutes later Dad came down the beach. He put his arms around her from behind and kissed the top of her wet head.

"Do you love storms?" he asked.

"They love me," said Zoe quietly. He'd have short

hair when she turned around. She'd let another strong gust blow up from the ocean before she turned back to see.

By midmorning the old Chevy van broke through the curtain of coastal rain and chugged north on the freeway. Zoe had a clear view of Dad up in the driver's seat. His hair didn't look too bad cut short, Zoe decided, but she wondered if he would miss it.

He and Mom were doing everything they could to find work, and Dad seemed real excited about the job interview today. But Oregon? She leaned against the window and watched the plump clouds overhead. Beside her Juke was threading a gummy worm between his toes and singing, "'Did you ever think when the hearse goes by that you might be the next one to die?'"

"Cut it out," said Zoe.

He wove a second worm through his toes, singing, "'The worms go in. The worms go out. The worms play pinochle on your snout.'"

"Disgusting!"

"Quiet, kids," called Dad from the front seat. "We're about to cross the Oregon border. Why don't you close your eyes and see if you can feel the minute we cross over."

Juke popped the gummy worm in his mouth, sucked it halfway in, and let the green end hang down to his chin.

Zoe closed her eyes. The seat belt tightened around her middle as she inched forward to plant her feet flat on the floor. The shocks on the van were zilch. If there was anything to feel while crossing the border, she'd know it. She gripped the seat, the smell of Juke's gummy worms flooding her nose. The van bounced and shuddered as they careened down the freeway. Zoe tried to concentrate, but her stomach felt like a yo-yo.

"Now!" yelled Juke.

"Nope," called Mom. "Not yet."

Suddenly there was a loud rapping noise, as if a group of angry trolls were stoning the van.

"Oh no!" shouted Dad. "Not now!"

Zoe opened her eyes as Dad pulled over to the shoulder. On the wet pavement behind them tire strips curled up in a line like snakes on parade.

"Oh, this is great!" fumed Dad. "Just great! I have to be at my interview in my suit and tie, looking fresh and cool, in two hours!"

"We'll make it," said Mom, swinging open her door. "We're lucky to have a good wide shoulder here, and the flat's on the passenger side."

"Can we get out?" asked Juke.

"Yes. But you and Zoe have to stay up on the hill while we change the tire."

They leaped out the door and climbed the hill together.

"Want my other worm?" asked Juke.

"No. That's okay." Zoe plucked a white blade of grass and bit down. The sweet, dry taste filled her mouth with summer. She pointed to the sign down the road. "Did you feel it?"

"Feel what?"

"The blowout happened the minute we left California. Like a warning."

Juke scratched his chin with a foxtail. "What kind of warning?"

"Someone doesn't want us here. In Oregon, I mean. We should turn back."

"What kind of someone?" said Juke, warming to the subject. "A green kind of someone all covered in puke-slime? Or a pale kind of someone with bloody fangs? Or—"

"Shut up, Juke."

Below them Dad was pumping on the jack, and the van was slowly tipping to the side like an old arthritic dog raising his leg to take a leak. Cars whizzed past, making the grass at the bottom of the hill dance. Then Zoe heard a siren screaming from somewhere down the freeway. She bit down hard on the dry blade. "See? What did I tell ya? Now the cops are after us."

The police car pulled up behind the van. A female officer stepped out. "You folks okay?"

"Fine," said Mom. "Just a flat."

The officer took in the old van. "Where are you heading?" she asked.

"Scout River," said Dad.

She adjusted her belt. "Good fishing up there. I caught a couple of trout last year."

Juke rolled his eyes. "Uh-oh."

Zoe and Juke beat it down the hill to intervene

before Mom launched into her "save the animals" speech.

"Well, actually," said Mom, "We don't indulge in—"

"I heard Scout River's got this great swimming spot," panted Zoe.

The officer tilted her head. "Yeah," she said. "Used to swim there when I was a kid."

Dad tugged the tire off the van with a grunt. The officer cleared her throat. "I see your tabs expire in a few weeks."

"We'll have to get an emissions test," said Mom with a nod.

"Doubt this old thing will pass," said the officer, glaring down at the rusty tailpipe.

"Oh," said Dad, tightening a bolt on the spare tire, "she runs like clockwork."

Juke tapped Dad's shoulder. "Dad, I gotta . . ." He glanced up at the officer. "I gotta you know what."

"We're almost done here, Juke. I'm sure there's a gas station down the road where we can use the—"

"I gotta go now!"

Zoe watched a bead of sweat trickle down her mom's neck as Dad lowered the van onto the spare and took apart the jack. Mom reached into the open door and pulled out the plastic jar wedged behind the seat. "Get in, honey, you can use this." Juke climbed into the van to take a leak in the empty mayo jar. A minute later he slid open the van door. A sleeping bag tumbled onto the pavement as he tried to shove the mayo jar into Mom's hands. "You can leave that in the van, Juke," said Mom, putting on a stiff grin.

The officer picked up the sleeping bag and handed it to Zoe. "Have a good camping trip," she said.

"Thanks," said Zoe hoarsely.

9

Dad raced across the college parking lot. "I got it!" he said, leaping into the front seat.

"Great!" Mom planted a big wet kiss on his cheek.

"It's just three nights a week right now," said Dad, "but if I can land that day job I applied for at the camping supply store, we're in like Flynn."

"I'll advertise for some housecleaning jobs," said Mom.

Zoe slammed *The Hobbit* shut. This was it? Scout River?

"Captain Flynn!" called Juke, still deep in the space battle. "We're under heavy enemy fire from Zorkus Three. Should we pull back? Over."

Dad turned around. "Stay put, Number One," he said through cupped hands. "Starship reinforcements are heading your way. We're not going to let Emperor Orkus Zorkus push us around anymore. Over."

Thunder boomed overhead and lightning flashed the van windows green. Zoe felt like she'd entered Smaug's dragon cave, only she didn't have Gandalf around to help her out. Wizards didn't usually hang out in college parking lots.

"Why don't we get some ice cream and celebrate," said Dad, starting the motor.

Zoe crossed her arms. Who wanted ice cream on a rainy day? She looked out the window at the steel-gray clouds. "Where's our house?"

Mom shot her a confused look. "What, honey?"

"If we're gonna be staying here, I want to see our new house."

Dad turned onto the road. "We'll find a place as soon as we've got first and last month's rent, Zoe. Did you see those little old houses on the edge of town, guys? One had a For Rent sign out front. Once the jobs are secure and the money's coming in . . . it's only a matter of time."

He started whistling his favorite Jam for Breakfast song. Zoe watched the line of wet houses snug up against the sidewalk as the van flew by. They passed row on row of shingled roof tops with smoke curling from the chimneys.

"It couldn't be better timing, Hap," said Mom from the front seat. "School starts next week."

Zoe pulled away from the window and clutched her seat.

"Looks like you'll both be going to Einstein Elementary School," said Mom, her eyes bright. "We passed it on the way into town. It's right across from Winslow Park, remember?"

"A school for geniuses," said Dad.

"Just a regular school," said Mom.

Zoe nodded, the words *School! No! Stop! Not yet!* bottlenecked in her throat. She wanted Dad to slam on the brakes. Stop the universe. No one had asked her if she wanted to go to Einstein. No one had asked her if she wanted to live in Oregon. They were five hundred miles from home, for gosh sakes! She'd seen the map!

"It's got a good-size playground," said Mom, coaxing Zoe from her sudden coma. Zoe couldn't move. Couldn't even blink. Her eyes felt dry as flashbulbs.

Zoe broke free from the trees and climbed a boulder as the sun edged above the high mountains. She could see the whole town of Scout River from this spot. Her eye wandered from the graveyard on the grassy hill below to the river strung like a giant's silver necklace along the edge of town. To the far right she could see the place where the river spilled into the sea. And looking the other way, maybe a half mile out of town, she spied a riding track. From her lookout spot, the horse running round the track looked no bigger than an ant. When she closed her eyes halfway, her eyelashes X-ed out the horse altogether.

As soon as Dad had gotten the teaching position, he'd scored the job at Henry's Camping Supply. Mom had advertised on local bulletin boards and found three housecleaning jobs. They were going to find a rental house or maybe an apartment as soon as the money started rolling in, as Dad liked to say, but for now they were hidden a mile out of town in the woods, camping out in the forest above the cemetery. No tent this time because they couldn't afford to be seen, so it was down to sleeping in the van each night.

Zoe never thought they'd end up here. Secretly, she'd thought Dad would give up his job search and they'd drive back to Tillerman. Once there, Dad would magically find a job (one he just hadn't noticed before) and they'd pick up their old life again. The whole summer would go down in the Flynn family record book as one long uptight camping trip. Some dreams were hard to let go of even when reality smacked you right in the face.

"Zoe?" called Mom. "It's time to go."

"Sure. Okay." Zoe jumped down from her perch and ducked back into the woods. Dad had already stashed the camp stove and pulled the bicycles off the rack.

"You're sure you and Juke want to ride down the first day?" he asked.

"Yeah," said Zoe, grabbing the handlebars. Mom jammed a lunch sack into Juke's backpack.

"Remember," said Dad, "the school's got my cell phone number in case of emergencies."

Juke pulled his bike up beside Zoe and got on. Mom found the hairbrush in the van and pulled it gently through Zoe's hair. "And they've got a P.O. box for our address until we're more settled in," said Mom. She paused to peer at Zoe more closely. "Did you brush your teeth?"

"Yep."

"Okay, kids," said Dad. "Go forth upon your mighty steeds and ride into the jaws of public education."

"Cut it out, Dad."

"Race ya," called Juke, and he started down the dirt road. Zoe pedaled with a fury till they'd passed the cemetery and hit a paved street that wound down Cascade Drive to the bottom of the hill. She raced down the road and across the bridge, flying so fast, she knocked over a flower wreath at the far end of the bridge. She skidded to a stop and got off her bike to lean the wreath up against the two-foot white cross. It looked like the cross had been there awhile, but she hadn't noticed it before. Somebody was taking care of the cross, though. Zoe could tell because the flowers on the wreath were still fresh and the photograph tacked on to the wood was clean. Under the photo the flower wreath read WE MISS YOU, JULIA. Julia flashed a crooked smile at Zoe from her photograph.

She was probably ten or eleven when the photo was taken. Dressed in shorts and a tank top, she stood on a sunny deck, Frisbee in hand, her short blond hair blowing across her cheek. Zoe had seen crosses on the side of the road before, so she knew what this one meant. Julia was dead. She died right here on this very spot. Probably hit by a car.

"Hey," called Juke, pulling up next to her. "I thought we were in a race."

Zoe climbed back on her bike. "Maybe we shouldn't ride so fast," she said.

"That's loser talk," called Juke, taking off again. They sped along the park road till Zoe's breath knifed through her lungs and sweat trickled down her back.

At the corner a cop car started to trail them. Zoe slowed down and pulled closer to the curb. Okay, so she'd pulled out of the bike lane to try to pass Juke. They didn't give you a ticket for that, did they?

"I won!" shouted Juke, skidding to a stop by the schoolyard. He popped off his helmet and locked his bike to the rack.

"Did you see the police car?"

"Yeah, so?"

"He was following us."

"Was not."

Zoe watched her brother stroll into the playground with all the confidence of a Jedi master. Why couldn't she walk like that, step into every new place like she owned it? She fumbled with her bike lock, laced the chain around the old frame and through her helmet. It was her turn to step through the schoolyard gate.

10

Kids streamed onto the playground.
They gathered into small groups, comparing their new
clothes, new shoes, new binders. Near the maple tree,
Zoe knelt down and jammed her hand into her backpack
to find her glass knob. If she had Bilbo's magic ring in her
pack, she'd slip it on her finger right now and vanish.
Whoosh! Free to walk in and out of classrooms unseen,
she could spy on the kids and teacher, determine the best
place to sit, figure out what kids to avoid.

Bilbo used the ring to hide from Smaug in the caves
of Lonely Mountain, but a new school was just as dangerous as Lonely Mountain. Okay, there weren't any
dragons here, but every school had kids who loved to set
dirty traps, tell cruel stories behind your back, and treat
a new kid to a thousand ingenious forms of playground
torture.

Someone blocked Zoe's sunlight. She froze midsearch

and looked up. A tall, slender girl peered at her, the morning light spilling gold down on her dark hair and skin.

"Lose something?"

"No." Zoe came to a stand. "Just making some adjustments."

"I'm Aliya."

"Zoe."

"Sixth grader?"

Zoe nodded.

"Me too. New in town?"

"I'm from Tillerman, California."

"Tillerman." Aliya said the word slowly, as if she savored the sound. "I've lived here all my life, but we flew over to Pakistan this summer to pick up my nanni, I mean my grandma. It was so hot over there, I thought I was going to die!"

The bell rang. Aliya turned. "Who've you got?"

"Ms. Eagle."

"Me too."

"Is she anything like her name?" asked Zoe as she followed Aliya into the stucco building.

"People say she swoops down on you from above when she's angry," said Aliya. "And you never know when she'll do it." Zoe couldn't tell if Aliya was teasing her because she couldn't see her face. She kept her eyes on Aliya's green backpack and long black braid as they wove their way through hundreds of kids to their classroom.

Light flooded from the ceiling, brushing the desktops

with yellow cream. The desks were arranged in groups of four, with name tags showing everyone where to sit. Aliya found her seat while Zoe hunted in the back, hoping for a desk by the door or at least close to the window. No such luck. At last she spied her name in the front corner of the room. The worst possible place. She'd have to face the teacher, keep her back to the class, and she couldn't even look out the window.

Zoe had learned most of what she needed to know about the social structure of her sixth-grade class by the end of the first recess. The most popular boys were Brad, Jamal, and Dylan. On the girls' side the most important sixth-grade survival tip was knowing that Mallory Smelser was on top. Mallory was the queen; everyone else was either friend or peasant, with the lowest peasant being Sheila Bellows because she was too poor to live in a house or an apartment and her family stayed in the trailer park on the edge of town.

Zoe registered this point right away. If Sheila was on the outs just because she lived in a mobile home, what did that make her? She'd definitely have to keep her living situation secret from everyone at Einstein. The only thing Zoe couldn't figure out was Aliya. Somehow she managed to live outside of Mallory's kingdom. Cool trick. Zoe wasn't sure how she pulled it off, but she hoped if she stuck close enough to Aliya, maybe some of her magic would rub off.

After math Ms. Eagle announced that the students

would all write an essay about how they spent their summer vacation. She smiled as she gave the assignment, as if she were the first teacher on planet Earth to think up this great idea. Zoe stared at her blank paper and felt her tongue go wooden in her mouth. Okay, she had two choices here. Tell the truth, which she couldn't do, or lie, which she didn't want to do. The light blue lines on the page began to move in and out like a TV on the fritz. She stood up suddenly, grabbed a rest room pass, and beat it down the hall.

At the drinking fountain she downed about a gallon of water. She had to think of a way around the stupid assignment, but her mind was mush. The water twirled in the white bowl and ran down the little metal holes at the bottom. She returned to class with a belly full of water and a brain on empty. Everyone was already writing, and the three titles she spotted as she headed back to her desk, said it all. Trish's: *My New Tree House.* Karl had printed *Dirt Bike Racing* across the top of his page, and Mallory's read *My Trip to Disney World.*

Zoe pulled out her pencil. Okay, she'd tell the truth about her summer, she'd just leave out the part about losing her home, her best friend, and her dog. Across the top of her paper she penciled *My Camping Trip.* She wrote about body surfing on the California coast. Cooking hot dogs over a beach fire at night. (So they were tofu hot dogs. Nobody had to know the details.)

Later that afternoon Ms. Eagle read some of the essays aloud to the class. Aliya's was first. Zoe put her chin in her hands and listened. The way Aliya described her month in Pakistan made Zoe feel like she was right there with her exploring the crowded bazaar with Aliya's grandmother. Buying colorful glass bangles and cloth shoes called *khusas* with golden embroidery. Tasting the cool mangoes and *kulfi* ice cream. Zoe could see the other girls looking at Aliya, wondering what it would be like to fly across the world and shop in an outdoor bazaar.

Ms. Eagle placed the essay on her desk and held up Aliya's drawing. Zoe cringed, waiting for the sound of laughter that was sure to come, but Ms. Eagle didn't ridicule Aliya's picture. She just held it up for all to view. There was the crowded marketplace, the stall with sparkling glass bangles next to folded silk scarves.

Zoe rubbed her sweaty hands on her jeans. Okay, so having your artwork held up for all to see didn't have to be a complete disaster. Just because Ms. Snell had blown Zoe's chance at any kind of cool by making fun of her pink moon in front of the whole class didn't mean it always had to be that way.

Next Ms. Eagle read Karl's essay on dirt bike racing. According to Karl, he'd won every race. Probably a big fat lie, but the class cheered anyway. Why not? The last essay she picked to read aloud was Zoe's. Zoe could hardly breathe as Ms. Eagle sped through her lines, but the magic worked. The other kids were giving her big-eyed looks, wishing they'd spent a few weeks camping at the ocean with nothing to do but swim, make sand castles, and toss the Frisbee.

Ms. Eagle looked up from the paper. "You left something out," she said. "Didn't you, Zoe?"

"What? No. I don't think so."

"I think you did."

All the eyes in the classroom were on Zoe. She could feel them drilling a thousand holes into her head. "We . . . we did a lot of camping. Like I said." Her mouth was so dry now, the insides of her lips were glued to her teeth. How did Ms. Eagle know they were living in their van? Had Juke already spilled his guts at recess? Zoe drove her fingernails into her pencil. The next time she got her hands on Juke, she'd pound him right into the—

"You moved, didn't you?" asked Ms. Eagle.

"Moved?" asked Zoe, as if it were some foreign word she'd never heard before. Giggles swept across the room. Zoe blushed.

"You're new in town. I take it you moved into a new home here this summer?"

"Oh, that!" said Zoe.

"Well," said Ms. Eagle, "it's a pretty big change, but I guess camping is more fun to write about." She piled the essays on her desk and passed out the new history books.

Zoe gripped her pencil. Close one. No one knew they were living in the woods. Not yet, anyway. A thin crack was rising up the side of the No. 2 pencil. Press it a little harder, and the stupid thing would break.

11

The cop had been following her again.
She'd biked through town, the patrol car moving slow in the traffic behind, until she'd turned onto Winslow Park Road. She pulled over to Julia's cross to wait. If he was following her, she'd call his bluff. Zoe licked her salty lips and checked out the new photograph tacked to the cross. Julia on horseback. She was smiling with her whole face. A big crooked smile, like she was about to say something funny when the picture was taken. Zoe wondered what she'd been thinking about in that one, bright moment.

She was still staring at that photo when the patrol car pulled up beside her. The cop rolled down the window, took off his sunglasses, and looked at Zoe. His eyes were blue and they had dark rings under them, the kind Dad got when he stayed up all night writing chapters for his books. She waited for him to say something. Maybe he suspected something was up with her. You couldn't tell a kid was homeless just by looking at them, could you?

Zoe wiped her sweaty hands on her jeans. The cop cleared his throat. His eyes watered. He rubbed them. Too much dust on the road. He put his sunglasses back on. Zoe saw two reflections of herself looking small and lost inside his silver shades.

"I was just, you know, checking out the new picture here," said Zoe, pointing to the cross. Silence. A bead of sweat dripped down the cop's upper lip.

"Well, I gotta be getting home," said Zoe. She restraddled her bike and rode across the bridge. It would have been better if the cop had said something, anything. His silence made her nervous. What was his problem, anyway? And why did he keep turning up? It wasn't like she was a criminal. People weren't arrested for living in their van, were they? It wasn't like they were hurting anybody or anything.

She pedaled harder. The cops here in Scout River were weird. Not like the nice cops in Tillerman, who helped you out when your bike got stolen by some high school creep. She would have never gotten her bike back last year if the cops hadn't found it in the ditch outside of town.

Zoe turned right and sped along the back river road. The sound of a car motor thrummed behind her. Well, if the cop was planning to dog her, he was in for a ride. She'd never lead him to their camping spot. He could follow her around town for a whole year if he wanted to, and he'd come up with zilch. She took on more speed, putting as much distance as she could between herself and their camping place.

If she were in Tillerman, she'd know where to go to lose him. There were tons of places to hide in Tillerman, like the big hollow redwood in Fletcher Park or the gnarled blackberry bushes by the water pipe where she and Kellen used to hide from Chris Tucker when he was in the mood to slug someone. No place like that here. She had to ride faster, harder, in case he was behind. She could hear the sound of an engine creeping up like a prowling cat behind her, but she didn't turn around. Too much of a freak out.

A row of houses to her left were squatting in the shade, their windows dark and their shingles all moss covered. *Ride more. Ride faster. In case he's still behind!*

The road split, and she veered right to speed along the river's edge. Ten minutes later she pulled over by a tall metal fence that surrounded a mobile home park. Must be the place the kids all talked about. The place where Sheila lived. She turned to look now, expecting to see the patrol car, but a small truck sped past in a flurry of wind and leaves. Maybe she'd really ditched him. If not, she could pretend she lived here in one of these mobile homes. Kind of a rough-looking place, though. Not at all like the mobile homes in Tillerman. The people who lived there had shiny old cars and flower boxes and neat little square lawns, which they kept as short as military haircuts. Most of the lawns here were long enough to lose footballs in. The trailer closest to her had a rusty dishwasher out front. Next door some kid's broken tricycle sat on a sagging porch.

Zoe was about to leave when she noticed a woman in one of the kitchen windows. Golden light shone inside, so even in the late-afternoon shade she could see the woman clearly. She was singing something as she worked over the sink. Zoe couldn't hear the song—she could see only the lady's mouth moving as steam rose from the faucet—but something about that window with the light coming through it made Zoe want to go inside that mobile home.

She wanted to get cozy in that kitchen. Maybe have a few graham crackers and a cup of cocoa. The woman tipped her head and plucked some leaves off the herb plant on her windowsill, and Zoe's chest started to ache. She pulled herself away from the scene and walked her bike along the side of the fence.

Across the yard a group of high school guys came outside to perch on the roof of a dead station wagon and light up some smokes. The red-haired guy took one look at Zoe and blew a series of smoke rings. Not the friendly sort of smoke rings Gandalf blew in Bilbo's house, but the "I'm cooler than you" sort of smoke rings guys blow when they've got something to prove.

Just then Sheila stepped onto a cluttered porch three trailers down. Zoe stood very still beside the bushes, hoping Sheila wouldn't spot her.

"Hey, baby sis!" shouted one of the boys. "Bring us a bag of potato chips!"

"Get it yourself, Mark," called Sheila.

"Bring the chips or I'll kick your butt!" shouted Mark. Sheila backed into her double-wide trailer home to grab the chips. Zoe should have left then and there, but something made her hang out by the bushes. She heard one of the boys snort as Sheila delivered the chips to her older brother.

Mark tore open the bag.

"Could I have one?" asked Sheila.

"Beat it!" yelled Mark.

Zoe thought about running across the yard, leaping onto the car, and dumping the chips on Mark's head. Some guacamole would have come in handy too. She'd like to dip his face in it.

Mark caught her watching him. "What are you starin' at?" he called. Zoe's legs felt as rubbery as licorice whips. Wrong time for her legs to wimp out on her.

"Hey, Zoe," said Sheila. She waved at her from across the yard as if Zoe were a rescue ship come to throw her a line. But when Mark and two other boys leaped off the station wagon and started heading her way, Zoe chickened out and hopped on her bike.

She raced down a narrow trail. Behind her she could hear the boys' feet pounding the dirt. The rutted path made riding hard, and she was going way too slow. Zoe fought against the dirt and roots, her front tire wobbling like some old lady doing a jig in high heels. She could have used the cop right now. He was broad shouldered. Strong looking. He could leap out in front of those tough guys and put his hand up in the air. They'd come to a dead stand under his amazing cop powers. But then, she'd done too good a job of ditching him. Now it was up to her stupid bike to make a getaway. Not much chance of that.

About a quarter mile down the path the guys slowed down as their lungs started to give out on them. One by one they leaned against the pines, coughing and spitting in the dirt. For the first time in her life, Zoe was grateful for the destructive power of cigarettes.

12

You could stand living in a funky old van if you spent most of your time anywhere but there. Zoe was pretty sure Mom and Dad felt the same way because they came up with a rock-solid evening schedule that kept the family warm, clean, dry, and active. Three nights a week Mom tried to keep Zoe and Juke busy while Dad taught his literature classes. Monday nights after dropping Dad off at the college, they hit the Laundromat. Zoe didn't mind hanging out there because it had a TV set you could watch sometimes. That is, unless old Mr. Numrich was there insisting they turn it to *Monday Night Football*. Tuesdays and Thursdays they hung out at the library till Dad was done with his class. Wednesday, Friday, and Sunday nights they all went swimming at the indoor pool. It cost the family four bucks to swim, but it was the only place they could take hot showers and wash their hair, so it was worth it.

Even with all of Mom and Dad's careful planning, living in the van wasn't working out. It was kind of like four turtles trying to share one shell, and Zoe was getting pretty sick of it. Regular things, like doing homework, were okay on library nights, but Zoe figured it would be easier to do homework in the monkey cage at the zoo than in the van with Juke bouncing around next to her.

On Wednesday night, her hair still wet from swimming, Zoe scrunched down in the backseat with her binder.

"Zeeuu! Pow!" cried Juke, flying his spaceship over the seat. "Watch out! We're under attack!"

"Quiet!" said Zoe. "I'm trying to work." She'd practiced her spelling words three times now, covering the tough ones, writing them, checking them again. *Number 8: eliminate.* E-l-i . . .

"Bam!"

"Stop it!" She'd like to eliminate Juke right now. Now, where was she? *Oh, yeah.* E-l-i-m . . . The space war going on beside her was blowing the letters right out of her head.

"Blast 'em! Boom! Nothing stops the lunar warrior!"

"I said, shut up!"

"Zoe," said Mom, "Juke's not hurting anybody."

"He's hurting me! I can't get anything done in this stupid van!"

"Juke, can you quiet down?"

"I'm coming in for a landing," said Juke. Mom turned back to her gardening book.

Zoe stared at the spelling page. *Okay, number 9: acknowledgment.* Zoe covered her book and started writing a-c-k . . .

"Boom!" called Juke. And that's when Zoe exploded. First her binder went down, then her book went flying and she pounced.

"Stop it, Zoe!" Mom lurched into the backseat to pry her off Juke but not before Zoe got in some good punches and Juke retaliated with three kicks to her shin.

That night Zoe lay awake in her sleeping bag, her brains on overdrive, trying to think of a way to ditch life in the van. Her heart was ticking like a time bomb. She needed out, and soon.

A week went by. Two. Still, she stared at the van ceiling every night trying to puzzle it out. Each time she tried to come up with a solution, she ended up with a headache.

As it turned out, the answer to their problem didn't end up coming from her head. It came from somewhere down in town when she skidded to a stop outside the minimart.

She shouldn't have taken the time to stop at all since she was on her way to her new job at Mrs. Garmo's house. But she was really thirsty, and she'd pulled her bike up to the window just to stare at the slushy machine. A fat kid in a bright green shirt was filling up a jumbo cup with every single flavor. Cherry on grape on watermelon. His mom paid the guy behind the counter. A good-looking, dark-haired guy stepped up behind her to buy a smoothie, but she made him wait while she bought a couple of Megabucks tickets. He tapped his foot and read the ingredients label on the smoothie bottle while she decided how many tickets to buy.

Zoe gripped the handlebars and put her nose up to the glass. The answer was right in front of her. She could play the lottery. If she won, they'd have enough money to ditch the van and find a place. Better still, if she won the big cash prize, she could head down to Tillerman and buy out the people who'd taken her house! Why not? Nobody would be brainless enough to pass up a million-dollar offer for an old two-story house, would they?

She could count on Mrs. Garmo for ticket money. Mrs. Garmo was going to pay her ten dollars a week to dust her living room and walk her poodles, Jinx and Tiddlywink. She could buy lots of tickets on her salary.

She was still thirsty when she pulled away from the minimart, but her new idea was better than a slushy. It was better than ten thousand slushies! Zoe barreled up the street, turned the corner, and sped past Jackson's Hardware. Once the money started rolling in, she'd be able to buy tickets all the time.

Sweat poured down her neck as she whizzed through Winslow Park. They wouldn't have to keep up this struggle trying to make it here in Scout River. They could move back to Tillerman and live there for all eternity on the rest of the cash. She'd never have to move again. The park blurred blue green as she raced along, all the colors of the park, the trees, and the sky kaleidoscoping together.

At 891 Blair Street she let herself in and made a bee-line for the bathroom, where she filled a paper cup seven times and drank until her parched throat felt cool. Her stomach grumbled for food. She drank more water to shut her belly up, then turned off the brass tap.

"Woof! Woof!"

Zoe came down the hall. "It's all right, girls," she called from the other side of the kitchen door. "It's only me. I've come for your walk."

There were skittering sounds from the dogs' toenails on the kitchen floor as Jinx and Tiddlywink danced about in anticipation. Zoe opened the door, and the dogs stormed out, one black, one white. Jinx made a flying leap into her arms.

Zoe laughed. "Oh! Such a guard dog!"

She'd been surprised when she first met the dogs, thinking all poodles were little. But these were standard poodles, and both were as big as Merlin, though not as chunky. Tiddlywink was standing at the kitchen door now.

"Wait a sec," said Zoe. There was a note with a rose across the top lying on the kitchen table.

Dear Zoe,

You'll find a snack in the fridge. I hope you like cheese sandwiches. The girls will need to go to the bathroom first thing, so walk them as soon as you can and leave the dusting for your return. Have a lovely walk!

Yours,
Hester Garmo

P.S. The rose is for you!

Wind blew across Zoe's back and leaves tumbled over her shoes as the car passed and headed around the corner. The streets were too narrow here. There was hardly any room to walk a dog or ride a bike. Probably why that girl, Julia, was hit down near the bridge. Jinx squatted to take a whiz just as a car drove past. Zoe looked up to the treetops to avoid the driver's glare. Kind of embarrassing.

The poodles led Zoe onto a little neighborhood trail. Fir trees whispered overhead, letting golden afternoon light fall between their branches. She passed a couple of fences, the large houses stealing pieces of the sky behind them. After climbing over a fallen branch, she stopped a moment to smell the air. Someone was baking. The aroma of apple pie mingled with the pungent smell of fir and pine. Zoe poked out her tongue to taste the air. Mom used to make apple pie like that.

She turned and tugged the leashes. "Come on, girls." Back at the house Zoe filled the dogs' water dishes and kissed each one on the top of their curly heads. She'd give Mrs. Garmo's rose to Mom.

Megabucks, here we come!

13

Rain pelted down, soaking Zoe's hair as she pedaled past the barbershop. It was a Wednesday, so she wouldn't be walking the poodles today. She'd been hoping to ride around and explore the length of River Road after school. There was a horse stable with a riding track on the far side of town she wanted to check out, but this storm was driving her straight to the library. Well, at least she could curl up in a big stuffed chair with her book.

Turning the corner, she sped past Pet Pals. She would have made it to the library in ten minutes flat if the window of the Scout River Realty office hadn't sucked her in. Skidding to a stop, she pressed her nose against the window. Under the sign that read WE'LL FIND THE HOME YOU'RE LOOKING FOR were photographs of four houses. Her eye landed on the top photo. A big house with large front windows. It looked a lot like

Mallory's three-story house, which was so huge standing out on the hillside that you could see it from the school-yard. The print below the photo read:

Beautiful View Home. Four Bedrooms.
Three Baths. Expansive Living Room. Family Room.
Three-Car Garage. Sale Price $600,000.

Zoe's toes curled. *Six hundred thousand dollars! Jeez!* That couldn't be right. How could anyone on the planet have that much money unless he was the president or something? She leaned in closer and checked the prices of the smaller, three-bedroom houses, those that were more like her home in Tillerman. Maybe they wouldn't be so outrageous. But one cost $300,000, and the other two were priced at $370,000. Zoe pressed her forehead against the cold glass, her breath misting the window so that the house photos were covered by her own personal fog. She wanted to get her home back. But the whole thing was impossible! What was a person supposed to do? Tug a stocking over her head, score some ammo, and rob a bank?!

A gust of wind blew against her back. She straightened up, blinked, and tucked a strand of wet hair behind her ear. There was no doubt about it now. Her only chance to buy back her home would be to win the Megabucks prize.

At the library she'd checked out the Megabucks rules on the Internet. For every dollar you played, you got two chances to win. But you had to be eighteen to buy a ticket. Kind of a problem. And so far she hadn't figured out how to get around that one.

It looked like the day was going to be a total washout, but right then the Pet Pals door clanged and Aliya came out hefting a sack of cat food. Her mother stepped outside and opened her umbrella.

"Hey, Zoe," said Aliya.

"Hey."

"This is my mother."

"Hello, Mrs. Faruqui."

"Nice to meet you, Zoe," said Mrs. Faruqui. The wind blew her orange scarf over her shoulder. She caught the silken corner and pulled it back around her neck.

"You're soaking wet," said Aliya. "Can we give her a ride home, Ami?"

"I . . . ," said Zoe. She looked into Aliya's dark eyes. "I lost my key, and I'm locked out of my house till my mom gets home," blurted Zoe, crossing her fingers to cancel out the lie.

"Oh," said Aliya with a frown. "Well, you can come home with us, then." She glanced up at her mom. "Can she come over, Ami? Please?"

Mrs. Faruqui pulled a cell phone from her bag. "Would you like to call your mother and ask if it's all right with her?"

Zoe dialed her dad's cell. Hard to get all the info across with Aliya and her mom standing right there, but she was careful not to give too much away. Dad was cool about her going to Aliya's, and they agreed to meet up at the library around five thirty. She gave the phone back to Mrs. Faruqui. Sometimes good things actually happen to people who stand outside in the rain.

At Aliya's house Zoe removed her shoes in the front hallway. Wow, it felt good to be inside a house again. She felt kind of like an impoverished princess who had stumbled into a magic castle. She took in the living room while Aliya hung up her coat. A big stuffed couch, round inlaid coffee table, two high-back chairs. The pillows on the chairs had embroidered elephants on them. There was a bookcase on the right and, next to that, a high shelf with a present on it. At least it looked like a present—anyway, something wrapped in beautiful cloth.

"My family Koran," said Aliya, nodding at the shelf. "Our holy book."

"Why do you keep it there?"

"The Koran is always kept on the highest shelf in the room."

"Oh," said Zoe. She wanted to ask if she could see the book; she'd explored lots of beautiful books in Dad's bookstore. Maybe the Koran had golden lettering on the cover. But as soon as she stepped around the couch, her feet discovered the warm Persian carpet and her belly did a flip-flop. The Faruquis' rug looked a lot like the carpet Grandma Nell had given Zoe's family. She ran her toe across the plush wine red wool and let her gaze fall into the intricate designs. A giant rose-window pattern in the middle, like the stained-glass window she'd seen at church, and on the edges diamond shapes touching tip to tip. She used to lay on the floor back at home and trace the shapes. If you squinted your eyes, the diamonds were wild horses stampeding across the sunset plains. And if you tipped your head, they were a row of tiny mountains covered in golden snow.

Beside her Aliya straightened the newspaper sections piled on the corner table. "My brother, Asif, never folds the paper," she said. "I think he leaves it on the floor most of the time." Zoe wasn't listening. For a moment it felt like she'd been here in Aliya's living room and back at home in Tillerman at the same time. A kind of time travel.

She was still lost in thought a few minutes later as they sat in the kitchen watching Aliya's grandma make their after-school snack. Nanni looked too young to be a grandma. She wasn't gray haired and wrinkled like Grandma Nell. Her dark skin was smooth, and her silky black hair pinned up in a bun had only a few gray streaks in it.

Nanni's tunic waved like butterflies flitting over a meadow as she rolled out a ball of dough at the kitchen counter. The long scarf that matched the tunic's pattern was neatly folded nearby. When the dough was round and flat like a *chapati*, she spread a spoonful of buttery ghee across the top, folded the dough into a square, and rolled it out again.

"You'll like *parathas*," said Aliya, jumping from her

chair. "They're really good with jam." She peered into the fridge. "Do you like strawberry or raspberry?"

"Sit down, Aliya," said Nanni. "I will cook." At the stove she turned the *paratha* over in the pan and added more ghee. The top puffed up.

The *paratha* was love at first bite. Zoe closed her eyes and let the sweet, buttery taste spill down the back of her tongue. It was almost as good as the doughnuts at O'Shea's Bakery back home in Tillerman. She opened her eyes again and found Nanni standing by the table, looking down at her.

"It's very good," said Zoe, wiping ghee off her chin. Nanni nodded, her brows tilting as she turned to whip up two mango shakes in the blender.

Zoe leaned over to Aliya. "Is she mad at me or something?"

"No. That's just her way."

Zoe finished her mango shake and was chewing on another *paratha* when Aliya's brother strolled in. She knew she'd seen him before, then she remembered where. He was the guy she'd seen buying a fruit smoothie at the minimart. Asif was tall and slim, and his skin was the same creamy brown shade as Aliya's.

He took a *paratha* from the plate and leaned against the counter chewing.

"Sit down!" scolded Nanni. Asif crouched against the wall and nibbled on a *paratha*. Zoe wanted to say something, but her mouth was full of dough and she couldn't seem to chew or swallow with Asif looking straight at her.

"This is Zoe," said Aliya. "You know, the girl I told you about."

Told what about? What had Aliya said about her? Zoe shoved the *paratha* over to the left side of her mouth and managed to squeak out a "Hi." Asif looked a lot older than his sister. Probably a high school senior this year. Now Zoe's heart was really starting to bang around in her chest. He shopped right where the lottery tickets were sold!

"Don't mind Asif," said Aliya. "He likes to sit on nothing and sleep on the floor. He thinks he's an ascetic."

Asif smiled at Aliya and kept chewing. Zoe wished she could spit her mouthful of *paratha* out—she couldn't talk with it in—but she couldn't seem to swallow it right now either.

"So you're the quiet type," said Asif. Then he rose up from the floor, kissed Nanni on the cheek, and left the kitchen.

"How old is he?" whispered Zoe.

"Eighteen," said Aliya.

Eighteen! She knew it!

"Why?" asked Aliya.

"No reason." Zoe looked out the window to hide the blush that was spreading up her cheeks. She wanted to ask Aliya what *ascetic* meant. It apparently had something to do with sleeping on the floor and not using chairs. Well, she slept on the floor of the van on the nights when she didn't get the backseat. Did that mean she was ascetic, like Asif? She hoped his being ascetic wouldn't keep him from buying Megabucks tickets for her.

Beyond the slick, wet deck sunlight pearled through the trees. The rain had stopped, and now the kitchen was so quiet, Zoe could hear the wind swirling outside the window. It was something like the view from her own kitchen window at home in Tillerman. The evergreen trees crowded together beyond the deck. Tall, green, and stately, they hovered above the roof, whispering magic spells only trees could understand.

Zoe watched the waving branches. She had to get back home to her own kitchen, her room, her closet. She was stuck here the way Dorothy was stuck in Oz, only she didn't have ruby slippers she could click together. She had a glass doorknob jammed in her backpack and a couple of bucks she was hoping to buy a few lottery tickets with.

When she turned away from the window, Nanni was staring at her again. But the frown had disappeared from her face, and her eyes had softened. "You are missing someone," she said with a nod.

Aliya nudged Zoe under the table, but Nanni had heard Zoe's longing as clearly as if she'd spoken her thoughts aloud. Zoe wanted to ask her how she'd done that, but Nanni was already sweeping excess flour from the cutting board. Flour sprinkled onto her tunic like snow in a meadow.

14

They climbed the stairway to Aliya's room. Zoe leaned against the door while Aliya hurriedly made up her bed. "Didn't think anyone would be coming over today," she was saying as she pulled up her shiny gold bedspread. Zoe didn't care about the unmade bed. Her palms were going all sweaty as she looked around Aliya's room. It was totally great. Next to her own bedroom at home, this was probably the most perfect kid's room she'd ever seen. There was a shelf crammed with books and a matching shelf next to it showing a cool collection of tiny painted boxes. In the corner by the window was a small oriental rug and giant pillows with little round mirrors sewn into the fabric. Zoe flicked on the light, and the mirrors blazed as golden as tiger's eyes.

Aliya tossed her stuffed lion onto the bedspread and turned around just as Zoe scanned the bookshelf. "Have you read all these?"

"Oh," said Aliya, "I'm always reading."

"Me too," said Zoe. She pulled down *Black Beauty*.

"In fourth grade I read anything I could with a horse in it," confessed Aliya.

"Wow, me too. Dad read this one to us in his bookstore."

"He owns a bookstore?"

"Not now. He used to co-own one."

"All those books to pick from!" said Aliya.

"Yeah." Zoe grinned. "It was great." She stepped back and licked her lips. There was this funny feeling in her stomach. She and Kellen had hardly ever talked about books, and here she was at Aliya's house for the first time, talking about one of her favorite things like they'd known each other always. She flipped through the pages of *Black Beauty*. She'd promised Kellen they'd be best friends forever. That wasn't going change just because Aliya liked to read.

Zoe crossed the room to check out the drawings of horses along the wall. They were good. Really good. A few of them showed a chocolate brown horse, but most were drawings of a black stallion with a white patch on his chest. She'd never been able to draw a horse, and it wasn't like she hadn't tried. "Are these yours?"

"Yeah."

"How did you do it? I mean, horses are impossible!" This was too good to be true. First the books. Now this.

"Oh, I didn't draw them. When I said they were mine, I meant that I own them."

"Oh." Zoe froze her expression so that her disappointment wouldn't show. She leaned in closer to read the words under one of the drawings: *My Ali Baba*.

Ali Baba, she silently mouthed. Must be the horse's name. She wondered if Aliya could introduce her to the artist. Then maybe she could solve the elusive "how to draw a horse" problem—that is, if she could ever find a place alone to draw. "So," she said, "who drew them?"

"Somebody," said Aliya. "A friend."

Zoe looked at the black stallion galloping over the green hills. That drawing of Ali Baba was almost as good as the horse on the cover of *Black Beauty*. "I'd like to meet her," whispered Zoe.

"Well, you can't!"

Uh-oh, she'd stepped into forbidden territory. Aliya twisted the bangle bracelet on her wrist.

"Did you get into a fight with her or something?" Zoe knew about fights; she and Kellen had gotten into some doozies.

"No. Her name was Julia. She's just someone I used to know."

A picture came into Zoe's head, like the turning of a kaleidoscope, and it brought a dizzy feeling with it. "The girl at the cross?" said Zoe. "I've seen her picture. She was your friend?"

Aliya sat down on one of the giant pillows. "I used to have her over when she wasn't playing with Mallory."

Zoe's eyes widened. "How could anyone be friends with you and Mallory at the same time?"

"I don't know. They both took riding lessons at Shepherd's Glen."

"The stable just outside of town?"

Aliya nodded. "Have you been there?"

"No, but I've seen it."

Aliya flashed Zoe a confused look, and Zoe blushed. She'd seen the horse stable from her lookout rock near the campsite. But she couldn't tell Aliya that. Zoe slid *Black Beauty* back on the shelf. "She was hit by a car, wasn't she?"

Aliya crossed her arms. "I don't want to talk about it anymore."

"I just want to know. I mean, she wasn't struck by lightning near the park or—"

"Yes," said Aliya. "She took the turn too fast on her bike and skidded into a car!"

"Sorry," said Zoe, sitting down beside her. "I just wanted to know."

Aliya took an inlaid wooden box from her shelf and pried off the lid. Inside was another box and another. Removing the lid from the smallest box, she plucked out a little blue friendship ring. She put it on, held it up to the light, then slipped it off again.

"Maybe I should take those pictures down," she said.

"Don't," said Zoe. She could hear her heart thudding in her ears. "Julia's horses are beautiful."

15

Three cats added up to one dog, Zoe decided. Aliya's cats were all white, all beautiful, but you couldn't pet one for very long before it darted off the bed for safer ground. So between the three cats you got about as much petting in as you'd get with one dog.

Aliya had gone downstairs for more food. The *parathas* had been great, but after talking about their favorite boy bands (Background Noise being the definite winner), shooting markers across Aliya's big wooden *caram* board, and arguing about whether Brad or Jamal was the most popular sixth-grade boy, they were ready to sneak some cookies upstairs.

As soon as Aliya left, Bijlee flicked her tail and darted down the hall. Zoe shouldn't have followed her, but she missed Merlin badly and Mrs. Garmo's poodles weren't around to pet, so Bijlee was the next best thing. Down the hall Bijlee scurried into an open door, and without thinking, Zoe stepped inside.

Asif was sitting on the floor looking through a pile of college catalogs. His room was spare. There was a dresser, a few shirts on hooks, a little table against the wall piled high with books and papers, and a stack of neatly folded blankets in the corner. On the wall near the window was a big poster of a mosque in Mecca.

Asif looked up as Bijlee darted past and hid under his table. Zoe blushed, then tried to back out of his room. She hadn't meant to barge in like that.

"It's all right," said Asif, crawling over to Bijlee. Zoe took another step back, thinking he was talking to the cat. "She's nice when she gets to know you," he said, lifting Bijlee into his arms and bringing her to Zoe. Zoe rubbed Bijlee's head tentatively.

"She likes it when you scratch her under the chin," he said. "Like this." He demonstrated, and Bijlee began to purr. "That's it," he whispered into the cat's ear. "That's what you like. Isn't it?"

"I saw you at the minimart," said Zoe.

Asif nodded.

"They sell Megabucks tickets there," said Zoe.

Asif gave her a "so what" shrug.

"Would you buy some for me?" asked Zoe. Wow, she couldn't believe how straightforward she was being all of a sudden, but Aliya might be back any minute with the chocolate chip cookies.

Asif put the cat down. "Why?" he asked.

Zoe jammed her hands into her jeans pockets. "I want to win," she said honestly. "I need money for this . . . this homeless family." Her heart was galloping now like a runaway horse.

Asif crossed his arms and looked out the window. Maple branches waved outside, soundless. "There are lots of homeless people in the world. "

"This family lives in an old van," said Zoe, blushing.

"They're lucky, then."

"Lucky? The van is cold, and it's way too small for them! And they have to shower at the swimming pool, for gosh sakes!" She stopped herself. If she didn't shut up, she'd blurt the whole thing out. How Mom and Dad had to cook dinner every night on a stupid camping stove and how she had to sleep on a puffy mat on the floor when Juke had the backseat.

Asif was frowning at her now. "How do you know so much about this family?" he asked.

"I . . . I just . . ." She was shaking now, and she crossed her arms in front of her chest in an effort to control it. "I know the girl."

"Oh? What's her name?"

"Kellen," said Zoe, crossing her fingers in her armpit to cancel out the lie. She wanted Asif to stop looking at her so hard. It was like he could see right through her.

"Well, Kellen's family has it pretty good," said Asif. "I saw a girl your age in Lahore. She was dressed in rags. No shoes on her feet. She had to beg on the street for her food. She and her family had to sleep in a doorway.

Nothing as nice as a van to protect them from the rain."
He bent down to pat Bijlee. "You wouldn't know how
bad it was unless you saw it for yourself."

"If you could just buy some Megabucks tickets for
me," said Zoe desperately, "I could help this family get a
home. All I have to do is win."

"Win what?" asked Aliya as she stepped into the
room.

"Cookies," said Asif, eyeing the plate.

"You don't need to win cookies," said Aliya. "You just
have to know where Ami hides them."

That night Zoe showered at the community pool. One of
the worst parts of living in the van was that there was no
way you could get clean without going public. There was
a huge shower room at the pool with fifteen shower-
heads, but luckily, the pool had two private stalls hidden
behind blue curtains. Zoe always waited for a private stall
because Mom expected her to remove her suit and have
a real soap-down shower.

She turned the faucet a notch higher. She'd had a good
time at Aliya's house after school, stuffing herself with
parathas and rolling marbles for the cats to chase. But she
wished Asif had said yes to the Megabucks plan. He was
nice about saying no, though. Kind of embarrassing to find
out that Muslims don't gamble and that the whole idea of
asking him to help out was pointless from the beginning.
If she'd known that, she would have just picked up Bijlee
and left his room before spilling her guts all over the place.

"Come on, Zoe," called Mom. "Don't waste water."

"I've still got shampoo in my hair," called Zoe.

She turned and let the hot water pound her back. Suds tumbled down her legs in small, white avalanches. The thing was, short of robbing a bank or winning the lottery, it was just about impossible for a kid to get their hands on enough money to buy a house.

16

On the first Saturday in October, Zoe stood in line at Galaxy Burgers. Pretty weird place for a vegetarian, but she was hungry enough to eat a ton of onion rings. And since Asif couldn't help her win the lottery, the Galaxy Game was the only shot she had to win the kind of cash she needed to move back to Tillerman.

It was the giant star-studded sign in the window that had first drawn her in. The silver letters read: PLAY GALAXY GAME! BLAST OFF INTO BIG CASH PRIZES! She'd skidded to a stop on her bike, the words *big cash prizes* flashing across her brain. The next thing she knew, she was through the fast-food door and wiping the sweat from her neck as she stood in line.

She figured she could buy two Galaxy meals a week on her poodle-walking money. That meant she had eight chances a month to win a million.

"Okay, what'll it be?" asked the frizzy-haired guy behind the counter.

"Um, okay, uh." She scanned the list. "You got any veggie burgers?"

Frizzy Guy leaned on the cash register. "Can you read the sign or what?"

Zoe felt hot flames burning up her neck. How many brain cells would it take for Galaxy Burgers to come up with a name for a vegetarian meal? They could call it the Venus Veggie Burger or something like that.

The kid behind her in line looked up from his Game Boy. "You gonna order sometime in this millennium?"

"Yeah, okay," said Zoe. "I'll take the Saturn Special. No mayo and no meat."

Frizzy Guy yelled out to the fry cook, "Saturn Special! Hold the mayo! Ditch the meat!" He rang up the charges. "You gotta pay for the meat," he said. "Even if you only eat the bun. That's policy." Zoe put her money on the counter and stepped aside for Game Boy Kid to place his order.

She leaned against the wall and looked out the window. The grocery store across the street was hidden behind a blanket of fog. The sun was probably shining down in Tillerman today. Kids were probably still going to school in their shorts. October days down in California were pretty mild sometimes.

Zoe tapped her foot and started adding up the reasons to leave Scout River. One, she hated living in the cramped old van. Two, she was blowing it at school, and her grades were dipping down into D territory. Three, Mallory was getting dangerous.

Mallory and the gang had seen inside the van last week when Mom picked Zoe and Juke up at school. Big mistake, but it had happened so fast, Zoe couldn't stop it. Juke slid the door open, and there was the wooden sleeping platform with sleeping bags and the box full of dishes and cooking pots, right there for everybody to see. Of course, Mallory, Kelly, and even Jamal had all passed by right at that very moment. Zoe couldn't slam the door fast enough. *Wham!* She could still see the weird looks on their faces as they sized up the contents of the funky van.

"Number sixteen!" called Frizzy Guy.

Zoe put up her hand, and he slid her Saturn Special across the counter. She took a seat at the corner table. Steam rose from her open sack, and she went after the onion rings. Seeing inside the van wasn't the only problem. Two days after that Ms. Eagle had the class hold a public market for their economics unit. People sold cookies and crafts, and everyone bought stuff with fake paper money. Zoe had done a pretty good business selling handmade bookmarks, but Mallory was the one who'd made the biggest killing, which was totally unfair because all she'd done was jam a jeweled turban on her head and wave her hands over a dumb-looking crystal ball. Anyway, the crystal ball was just some upside-down glass candleholder.

Zoe never would have paid to get her fortune told if

Aliya hadn't dared her to. First Mallory pulled out some playing cards, turning over the nine of clubs and the three of diamonds. "You will take a long journey," she said.

Zoe shrugged. No duh. She'd already taken a long journey. "Anything else?" she asked.

"I need more money first." Zoe put her fake bills on the table. Mallory swept the bills into her cigar box, then gazed into her crystal ball. "Hmm," she said. "Something very big is going to happen to you in the future. It's coming clear now."

Zoe scooted to the edge of her chair. Kids behind her pulled into a tighter circle to listen.

"Ah!" said Mallory, her eyes narrowing. "I see your future in my magic crystal." She waved her hands over the ball. "You will meet someone famous and scrub her toilet!"

A shock wave of laughter hit Zoe from behind. Cheap shot. Mallory must have found out about Mom's house-cleaning business. If she'd figured out that much about Zoe's secret life, what else did she know? Zoe stared into Mallory's blue eyes. She should have retaliated, said something really raw to Mallory. Instead, she just sat there, dumb as a lawn ornament.

She was still thinking about the victorious smile that had spread across Mallory's face when she finished her burgerless burger. The fake cheese tasted like a milky paper towel with a little salt added for flavoring. Nothing but a napkin at the bottom of the bag now, and under that . . . She reached in and pulled out the Intergalactic Game Card. Her hands went all sweaty. She took a breath and cooled her throat with the shake.

With the taste of chocolate in her mouth, she leaned against the orange seat and lost herself to dreams. It would go like this. She'd win the money right away. And before long they'd all be back home in Tillerman. Mom would put on some more weight and act all happy again. Dad would have all the time in the world he needed to work in his study above the garage writing his new sequel book, *The Wizards of Morenth*. And she and Juke would pick up their old life right where they'd left off. She'd hang out with Kellen, snuggle with Merlin, close the door of her dreamroom and draw, draw, draw.

"Number eighteen!" came over the loudspeaker. She opened her eyes and braced herself against the back of her chair.

Now!

Zoe scratched the Intergalactic Game Card with her fingernail. The words *Need more rocket fuel* came up. She ripped up the card and dropped it in the bag.

17

Jinx and Tiddlywink led Zoe over the bridge, past Julia's cross, and into the far side of Winslow Park. They'd been out walking for an hour already, and she should be heading back to Mrs. Garmo's, but the poodles were tugging hard on their leashes and she wasn't ready to turn around. She had to find the perfect place to sit alone and read the letter she'd found in the P.O. box after school today. Kellen had finally written back!

Halfway up the trail Zoe stopped behind the library to pluck a few blackberries. October was way past the season and most of the berries were shriveled up like raisins, but some of them tasted okay. Jinx wagged her tail and poked her nose under the bush while Zoe chewed. You could pretend you were eating some of that expensive fruit leather kids like Mallory and Trish had in their lunch sacks if you thought about it hard enough.

The farther they walked, the wilder the woods became, and as the houses fell away behind them and the fog rose up from the river, Zoe could have sworn the dogs were leading her out of Scout River and straight into Mirkwood. Any minute a hobbit might pop out from behind a fir tree.

The path strayed away from the river, venturing into dense forest. The fog was even thicker now, but Jinx and Tiddlywink tugged her onward. The towering evergreens and the giant bushes with leaves the size of dinner plates made Zoe feel very small. Like she were no bigger than Bilbo.

At last the trail leveled out. She could still hear the road across the river, and she pretended that the sound of the passing cars was the sound of rushing water. She stopped to toss a handful of stones into the water. Rings grew outward and broke against each other. The deep part of the river was pale with the fog hovering over it, and the pines reflected in the water looked like a giant's finger painting on gray paper. The painting changed when a hawk's reflection sped across the river.

She bent to tie her shoe, then followed the hawk as it flew downriver away from the world. She was so intent on the bird's silent flight that she didn't see the abandoned cabin hidden in the bushes till Jinx stopped to take a sniff.

The cabin was about twelve feet by fourteen feet, all made of giant logs with moss growing on them. She stepped forward and slowly put out her hand.

The wind whispered—Grandma's voice echoing in her ears. *Find the door.*

This door was made of old wood, and it had a rusty knob. Taking a breath, she turned the knob and pushed. The old hinges groaned like a sound effect in a monster movie. Juke would have given it ten points on the scary noises scale. Tiddlywink whimpered and sat outside, but Jinx bravely sniffed the corners of the cabin while Zoe looked around. An old cobweb-covered chair leaned against the wall, but the cabin looked okay otherwise. No rotting smell or rat's nests. The windows weren't even broken.

Zoe scanned the woods outside for a pine branch she could use as a broom. Across the river a police car drove past. It was a cop car, wasn't it? By the time she looked up to see, it was too far gone to tell. *Lighten up,* she told herself. *You're starting to see things.* In a small clearing she found a fallen branch and came back in to sweep the cobwebs from the corners. She coughed as she worked, but she kept moving. Tiddlywink got her nerve up and trotted in to chase the swinging pine branch across the room. Jinx barked and ran in circles around her feet.

"Good find, isn't it?"

Tiddlywink wagged her tail.

"It's just like when Snow White found the cabin of the seven dwarfs, only that cabin was full of furniture and dishes and stuff." Jinx scratched her ear. "But that cabin was a mess just like this one, and she had to clean it up before she could sit down and take a rest." Zoe tossed the pine broom outside, shut the door, and knelt on the floor with the poodles to look out the front window.

It wasn't like her dreamroom at home. No bright yellow beanbag chair to curl up in. No shelves crammed with her favorite books. But it was a solitary place with a door that shut and a window that looked out on the water. The dust on the glass softened the view outside, making Scout River and the woods beyond look like a hundred-year-old photograph. Zoe rubbed Jinx's curly head and breathed in the dry-dust smell. She hadn't been able to shut the world out like this since she'd left her dreamroom at home.

If she had her drawing pad, she might be able to sit and draw here. It was a good alone spot. She could draw the wide, flowing river. The trees casting black shadows along the wavering surface. She felt that familiar tingling in her fingers. It had been a little over three months since she'd pulled out her chalks and done some sketching. That was way too long to keep her hands from moving across a clean blank page. Maybe she could come back here and bring her stuff next time. Anyway, at least she had something special to read, and it was waiting right in her coat pocket. She opened the envelope and pulled out Kellen's letter.

Hi, Zoe,
Scout River sounds awful! And Mallory sounds really snotty! I wish you were back in Tillerman.

Zoe looked up. Maybe she should tell Kellen about the Galaxy Game and her plans to buy back her house.

But then, Kellen didn't know she and her family were living in the van; she'd kept that secret to herself.

I didn't get to do the perfume thing like we planned because Chris punched out a fifth grader the first week of school and got suspended. Otherwise, things are about the same except for there's this new girl, Carla, who's really nice.

Zoe chewed her fingernail. *Carla, huh?*

Asif sounds too old. Check out the seventh- and eighth-grade boys. Carla and I went over to the junior high after school and saw a couple of cute guys on the soccer team. One of the boys came over and talked to us! He thought we were seventh graders, so we didn't tell him we weren't!

See ya soon,
K.

P.S. Writing letters takes too much time. Try to get e-mail.

Zoe stood suddenly, and Jinx leaped up to follow. "Stay!" she said.

Outside, she wrapped Kellen's letter around a big

rock and hurled it into Scout River. *Thunk!* Okay, it was environmentally incorrect and Dad would have gotten on her case, but she didn't care. The letter sucked, and she never wanted to read it again. First of all, what did Kellen mean by saying Asif was too old when she'd had a crush on Matt Kinsey last year and he was sixteen and already driving a car? And second, what was the deal with this new girl, Carla?

In the cold gray water Kellen's letter tore away from the rock. It rose ghostlike, then slowly spun round and round as it drifted downstream. Zoe watched the paper haunt the river, her fingers curling to a fist.

You could yell at a person who lived right next door to you. You could have a fight, then make up and be sharing secrets the very next day. She and Kellen had been doing that since preschool. But you couldn't fight with someone who was five hundred miles away. You just had to suck it in, put it on hold, while some other kid moved into your town, stole your best friend, and started living the life you left behind.

18

A skeleton ran along the sidewalk as the van chugged up Lyndon Street to Aliya's house. Dad hummed to himself as he turned the corner. "Just one more paycheck, kids," he said, "and we'll have enough for first and last months' rent. What do you say we go house hunting this weekend?"

"Sure," said Juke, his alien antennas bobbing as he nodded.

"Sounds wonderful," said Mom.

Zoe clung to the cardboard box in her lap. If this were a story instead of real life, she would have already won the Intergalactic Cash Prize and they'd be heading home to Tillerman right now instead of talking about a rental here in Scout River. Take *Charlie and the Chocolate Factory*. Charlie had to open only four Wonka bars before he found the golden ticket. Count 'em. Four. This week she'd be buying her ninth Saturn meal. That was five more chances than Charlie had, so she had to win soon.

"Here we are," said Dad, pulling to a stop at the top of Aliya's long driveway. "We'll pick you up at nine thirty."

"Stay in this neighborhood," reminded Mom. "And stick to houses where Aliya knows the people."

"I know," said Zoe. "We'll be careful."

"Hurry up, Zoe," said Juke, "or I'll be late to Gabe's house."

"I'm going as fast as I can." Zoe stepped over the rolled-up sleeping bags, yanked her computer costume out, and slammed the door. The van pulled out of sight in a cloud of blue smoke. She slid into her costume and tottered down the driveway.

The box slipped from side to side, and the cellophane computer screen made all the house lights blurry. Grabbing the banister, Zoe negotiated the long flight of stairs leading to the door, reached though the armhole in the box, and rang the doorbell. Her teeth chattered as she waited on the front porch, a stray wind blowing up inside her cardboard box. At last Asif answered the door with a big bowl of candy. "Oh, it's you," he said, bending down to peer through the cellophane screen.

Jeez, why did Asif have to be the one to get the door? Now he was sure to think of her as a little kid. She was a sixth grader. Maybe even too old to be trick-or-treating. At least she should have worn something beautiful and exotic; but there was no money for a costume, so she'd used the box she'd found behind the library.

The cardboard mouse and keyboard swung back and forth on their strings as she came into the kitchen. Aliya was standing on a chair while her mother stitched the hem of her water sprite dress. It was a knockout costume, blue green as a mountain lake, and the whole thing was covered in sparkles. "I'll be ready in a minute," said Aliya.

"She should not go out," said Nanni from her chair in the corner.

Aliya stepped down. "I'll be safe, Nanni. Aba will be with me."

"I don't know what this is. This going to strangers' houses on a cold night," said Nanni. "And they give the children candy, with no way to know if their hands are clean!"

Mrs. Faruqui put away her sewing box. Everyone seemed tense, as if the ghosts and goblins roaming the streets outside tonight were somehow real.

The kitchen clock ticked a raw, dry sound. No one moved. What was this, an old rerun of *The Twilight Zone*? Finally Mr. Faruqui came into the kitchen and took a flashlight from a drawer. "Shall we go now, children?"

"Yes, Aba." Aliya went to the coat closet with Zoe. "Nanni isn't happy here in America," she whispered. "She's always complaining."

"Why doesn't she go home?"

"She can't. Her home is here with us now."

"But if she's so unhappy—"

"Shh!" said Aliya. "Here she comes."

Nanni put a wool scarf around Aliya's neck. "You will wear this," she said. "I don't want even the wind to touch your cheeks." She turned around to peek through the cellophane computer screen. "And, Zoe. You have a coat on too?"

"Yes, Nanni."

"I don't know why you are going outside like this. I can make sweets for you here!"

"You can make some sweets for me," said Asif. But Nanni walked right past him.

The chill air hit them as soon as they walked out the door, and the branches of the thin maple rattled in the wind. They went up one street and down another, collecting candy door-to-door while Aliya's dad waited in the half-lit driveways.

Back on the street a pirate ran past followed by three tall ghosts. "The Martini brothers," said Aliya. "They usually steal Halloween candy from the little kids when the grown-ups aren't looking."

"Why do that when they could go door-to-door?"

Aliya shrugged. "It's what they like to do."

At a big three-story house Zoe reached past the hanging skeleton and pressed the doorbell. A green alien offered them Mountain Bars and Pixy Stix. Back up on the driveway Mr. Faruqui waited near a scarecrow.

"In Tillerman, Kellen and I used to come home with

shopping bags full of candy." Zoe swung open the brown picket gate for Aliya. "Mr. Swedenborg used to give the kids giant Milky Way bars, and if you made it to the Donovan house early enough, they'd give you a can of pop. Any kind you wanted!"

"Oh." Aliya stepped around a large rubber Frankenstein near the front door of the next house. Zoe touched the fake blood on his rubber mouth while Aliya rang the bell. The door flew open, and a six-foot Dracula offered them a choice of Milk Duds or Red Vines.

Eight houses later Zoe felt inside her bag as she walked up the road. Not even half full yet. They'd have to speed up if they were going to score enough candy to fill their bags before nine P.M. Kellen had probably already been to the Donovan house to choose her pop. She and Carla would be circling Manor Hill Drive, where the rich people loaded you down with candy. Their sacks would be totally bursting by now. Scout River was turning out to be slim pickings compared to her hometown.

They passed two witches yelling at a kid dressed as a jack-o'-lantern who was stooped over trying to tie his shoe. One witch had her hands on her hips, the other was wielding a spell wand. Zoe cracked up. "Kellen and I used to dress up as witches," she said. "We always had the same stupid paper hats and black dresses and magic spell wands made out of chopsticks painted silver." She sighed inside her cardboard box. "Tillerman's a great place to do Halloween."

"You live here now," said Aliya.

And just like that, Zoe's mood capsized. She looked at Aliya through her fake computer screen. "What's the deal with you tonight?"

A ghost drifted past.

"Nothing."

Zoe stopped. "Yeah, right."

"Come on, let's just go."

"Not until you tell me what's up."

"Sometimes I wonder if you really live here."

"What do you mean?"

"It's always Kellen this and Kellen that! Tillerman this and Tillerman that! What's wrong with life here in Scout River?"

"Nothing's wrong with Scout River, it's just . . ." She wanted to say—*I'm living with my whole family all cramped inside a stupid van! I used to have a house, a room of my own!*—but the words jammed up so fast inside her mouth that she skidded into the only lame words she could find: "It's just not the same as Tillerman."

Aliya swung around and started walking faster.

"Hey, wait up," called Zoe.

Aliya adjusted her crown as she walked. "School's better there. Halloween's better there. You're just like my nanni when she talks about Pakistan. You hate it here."

"I didn't say that!"

"You say it all the time! I invite you to my house, and I share everything I have. Nothing is good enough."

"That's a lie!"

Mr. Faruqui ran up behind them. "Aliya, Zoe, quiet. You'll disturb the neighbors." He put his hand on Aliya's shoulder. "You girls are supposed to be friends," he said. "Now, what is troubling you?"

Zoe watched a Tootsie Roll wrapper blow past. Aliya took off her green crown. "It's getting cold out."

"Do you want me to take you home?"

"Yes, Aba."

19

"**W**ow!" said Juke as he climbed into the van. "That was great! This trailer park's the best place in the world to trick-or-treat!" Most of his green makeup had been smeared off, and one of his antennas was missing, but he smiled as he dangled his plastic bag in front of Zoe. "I really scored. How about you?"

"Yeah, I scored big," said Zoe. She peered out the window as they pulled out of the trailer park. Someone had put a jack-o'-lantern on the roof of an old station wagon. The candle flickered in its laughing mouth.

Zoe unwrapped a Sugar Daddy and started sucking. The worst Halloween ever, and that included the time she'd gashed her knee falling down Mr. Hall's garden stairs. It was weird how Aliya had yelled at her, like she'd been the one who'd spoiled the fun. And then Nanni was so happy to see them back that she cooked up some homemade *barfi*, which sounded weird to Zoe but turned out to be this really good Indian candy. A white milk fudge with nuts in it. It was better than most of the junk she had in her bag now. She'd sort of made up with Aliya after eating Nanni's candy, but her stomach still felt tight from the fight.

Juke fished around in his bag. "Oh no!" he said. "Can we go back to Gabe's? I left some of my candy there!"

"We're already on our way home," said Dad.

"Well, I gotta get that stuff! What if he gets into my marshmallow bars and—"

"Just a sec, Juke." Dad turned to Mom. "You hear that noise?" The van was shaking more than usual. They drove across the bridge, then there was a sudden *snap,* followed by a thunderous drumming sound, as if Godzilla were using the van as a bongo drum.

"What now?" shouted Dad. He pulled over to the side of the road.

"What is it, Hap?" asked Mom.

Dad leaped outside, slammed the door, and inspected the engine. "Jeez!" he shouted. "I can't believe it!" Now they were all out of the van, looking at the engine.

Zoe tried to ask a question, but her teeth were cemented to her Sugar Daddy. After a while a kid and her dad came by, both dressed as clowns.

"Hey," said the dad. "Are you gonna need a tow?"

"Looks like it."

The clown bent over in his voluminous polka-dot

pants to check out the engine with Dad. "Looks bad," he said. "You want I should call it in?"

"That's okay," said Dad. "I've got my cell phone with me."

After the clown and his kid left, they talked about their options. Couldn't sleep outside tonight with the heavy rain clouds hanging overhead.

"I don't want to spend the money we've scraped together for rent on a motel room," said Dad. "It'll set us back."

"May I have one?" asked Mom, holding out her hand to Juke. Juke gave her a red sucker, and she popped it in her mouth. It wasn't like Mom to eat candy, but then, she was pretty stressed out right now.

"I know a place," said Zoe.

"What kind of place?" said Dad.

It took another twenty minutes for the tow truck to arrive. By that time they'd packed up their night gear, pulled out their sleeping bags, and taken the bikes off the rack. Zoe sucked the Sugar Daddy right down to the stick as she watched the front half of the van rise up into the air. Talk about the dead rising from the grave.

"Need a lift?" asked the driver.

"We can walk from here," said Dad, looking hard at Zoe. Zoe nodded reassuringly. The abandoned cabin wasn't far from here. She ripped open a package of jelly beans and popped one in her mouth as the tow truck pulled away. It's not often you get to see your whole house hauled off to the gas station by a tow truck.

They spent the night in the abandoned cabin while the rain pounded on the roof and the wind rattled the window. The floor was hard, but it was good to have a dry place to sleep. Juke was out like a light pretty quick, but Zoe lay on her back staring at the ceiling. Hard to sleep with the wind wailing past the window. A sudden gust along the outside wall made the bike chains rattle. A perfect Halloween sort of sound. Better than the fake recordings people played to spook the trick-or-treaters. Zoe shut her eyes, watching the candy-colored lightshow in her head. Beside her Mom and Dad were whispering.

"I can't believe this," whispered Mom. "We've worked so hard."

"Let's hope it's nothing major."

"What if it is?"

Zoe opened one eye a slit and saw Dad put his arm around Mom. "I've got to bring in the money faster. There's a possibility of some more classes at the college."

"But you've already got two jobs."

"I've got to get us into a house, Sadie."

"Maybe we should get rid of the van."

"Can't yet. We still need it."

Mom rolled closer to Dad. "What do you think of this place?"

"Okay for a day or two maybe. It looks abandoned, but somebody might still own it." Dad ran his hand through Mom's hair. "How are you holding up?"

"I'm all right. It's just, the kids—"

"I know."

Zoe turned over and the whispering stopped. In the morning Dad would put his "we can make it" face on again. Mom would work up a smile for her and Juke. But Zoe knew how much they wanted out. How much they wanted to get back into a home.

At eight in the morning Dad left for the gas station to check out the van, and Mom got ready to head off to a grocery store.

"I'll be back in about an hour with some healthy food," said Mom. "Hopefully, the problem with the van won't be major and we'll have it back sometime today." She threw on her coat. "You kids going to be all right?"

"Sure," said Zoe. "I've got *A Wrinkle in Time* to read and Juke's got *My Father's Dragon,* don't you, Juke?"

"Yep," said Juke sleepily.

A gust of wind ripped the door out of Mom's hand when she opened it. Mom struggled to grab ahold of it again. "Take care of your brother, Zoe, and stay here with—"

"I know. Stay here with the stuff." Mom looked a little hurt standing in the open doorway. Maybe Zoe shouldn't have finished the sentence for her. "Anything else, Mom?" she asked.

"Don't eat too much candy."

"Yeah, okay."

Mom heaved the door shut. Zoe sat up in her sleeping bag and felt around inside with her bare foot till she found the glass doorknob. While Juke hunted through his candy stash, she pulled the knob out and went to the window.

Pale morning light fought with swaying trees for a chance to lie down on the river. Zoe held the doorknob to her chest and caught a single ray of sun in the glass. If she closed her eyes and turned it to the right, just so, she could pretend she was opening her closet door. She could walk into her dreamroom, close the door, and be herself again. Zoe at home.

"What's up?" asked Juke through a mouthful of candy.

"Nothing." Zoe wrapped the knob in her T-shirt and slipped back into her sleeping bag.

Juke tossed a Tootsie Pop wrapper across the cabin.

"Hey, that's littering."

"Show me the garbage can!" He shoved the Tootsie Pop in his mouth. Zoe took a deep breath. She wanted to slug him, but that's what he wanted her to do, slug him so he could cry. She could always tell with Juke—his nose turned red right before he cried. It was turning red now, and she could feel her own eyes prickling with tears. Well, she wasn't going to let it happen. "You want me to read to you?" she asked suddenly. Juke nodded and pushed his book across the floor.

Zoe thumbed through the pages.

"Where are you?"

"He just met seven tigers."

"Oh, yeah." Zoe sighed. "I remember that part." She finished the chapter and began the next, reading all the way through the part where the rhinoceros picks the boy up on his horn and tosses him into the wading pool. "'Don't you know that's my private weeping pool?' said a deep angry voice."

She turned the page, then put the book down.

"Keep reading," said Juke.

"I can't. It makes my throat hurt."

"This sucks."

"No kidding."

"I wanna go home," said Juke suddenly. Zoe stared at Juke's red nose. Tears started running down his cheeks. He tried to hide them with a candy wrapper.

"Cut it out," said Zoe, "or you'll be needing your own private weeping pool."

"I can cry if I want to," said Juke. "I'm just as sick of living in the van as you are. Mom and Dad lied to us! They said we'd have a place by now!"

"They didn't lie. We had enough for a place before the van broke down."

"Yeah, well, I think we'll be stuck living in the van forever."

"No way!"

"Shut up!" Juke tossed another balled-up candy wrapper into the corner. He sniffed, trying to fight back more tears. Zoe pulled a juice box out of her stash. "Here, drink this. It'll make you feel better." She felt stupid saying that. She wanted to say, *Don't worry, I'll fix things up for us.*

I'll get our house back. But she couldn't make a promise like that. So far the Galaxy Game had been a bust, and all she had left from Mrs. Garmo's pay was about four bucks.

"Okay," she said. "I'll read to you some more."

They shouldn't have left their bikes outside the cabin where people could see them from the road across the river. But Zoe was too wrapped up in *My Father's Dragon* to think about that, so she was surprised to hear someone knocking at the door a little while later and even more surprised when the person on the other side turned out to be a cop.

20

It wasn't just any cop standing in the doorway. It was the policeman who'd followed Zoe the first day of school. The same one she'd ditched last month. She looked into his mirrored sunglasses and shivered.

"Morning," he said hoarsely. Steam rose from the paper cup in his hand, and for a moment Zoe imagined he'd stopped by to bring them some coffee. "I'm Officer Bergstrom, and your names are?"

"I'm Zoe and this is Juke."

He looked around. "What are you kids up to?" he asked.

"Reading," said Zoe.

"Camping," said Juke. Zoe cringed.

"Just pretending," said Zoe. "You know. Pretending to camp. For fun. You know."

Officer Bergstrom ran his fingers through his short

blond hair. He nodded at the sleeping bags and day packs full of clothes. "Looks like you're pretty settled in," he said.

"Not really," said Zoe, rolling up her sleeping bag awkwardly. She tried to tie the strings around the bag, but her hands were shaking so much that she couldn't control her fingers.

"Who else is in the game?" asked Officer Bergstrom.

"What?"

"Who else is pretending to camp with you?"

"No one," said Zoe before Juke could yank the Tootsie Pop out of his mouth and say, *Mom and Dad.* The officer eyed the extra sleeping bags.

"We thought it might be cold," said Zoe.

"You'll have to leave," said Officer Bergstrom. "This cabin's not safe. Should have been boarded up years ago." He walked to the corner. The boards under his black shoes creaked as if to affirm his opinion of the place. "Wood rot," he said. "You're lucky you didn't fall through." He looked at Juke. "Your parents know you're here?"

"Sure, they—"

"We're just playing," said Zoe. "I told you."

"I heard you, Zoe," said Officer Bergstrom. "I'm asking your brother."

Juke pulled the Tootsie Pop out of his mouth. "They know," he said truthfully. Zoe wanted to slug him.

"Well," said Officer Bergstrom. "Let's get this stuff out of here. I'll take you home."

"You can't," said Juke.

"We can walk," said Zoe quickly. "I mean, take our bikes," she corrected.

Officer Bergstrom peered out the doorway. A light rain was falling. "You've got a lot to carry on those bicycles," he said. "You'll ride with me so I can talk to your parents."

They took their stuff down the trail, crossed the footbridge and walked to the patrol car. Officer Bergstrom crammed the bicycles into the trunk while Zoe and Juke climbed into the backseat.

"What are we gonna do?" asked Juke.

"Shut up and let me think," whispered Zoe. But she couldn't think. Her brains felt about as useful as a wad of day-old bubble gum.

Officer Bergstrom started the engine. "Which way?" he asked. Zoe pointed straight ahead. What was she supposed to do? Lead him to the woods above the cemetery? They passed the library and the school. *Think!*

"Where now?" he asked. Zoe suddenly wanted to tell him to head to the freeway and drive about five hundred miles south to Tillerman. If he wanted to take them home, she'd let him. But the words caught inside her throat, and all she could manage was a small squeaking sound. "Turn right," she squeaked.

Where should she take him? The trailer park? Too late. They'd already passed the turnoff. They reached the bridge, and Officer Bergstrom pulled over beside Julia's cross. "Just a sec," he said, hopping out and slamming the door.

"What's he doing?" asked Juke.

"Fixing the ribbon," said Zoe. She watched him retrieve the fallen ribbon and reattach it to the cross.

"Must be a neat freak," said Juke. A minute later they were heading back up the road.

"Which way?" said Officer Bergstrom.

"Left," said Zoe. Wait. They were on Cascade Drive. In another mile they'd reach the woods above the cemetery. What was she doing?

"Turn right here," said Zoe. She should have taken him to Aliya's. Aliya would have covered for her. But her house was all the way across town. Brainless to think that would work, anyway, because he'd never believe they lived with Aliya's family. *Think!* What she really needed was a cozy little house with an actor and actress who could pretend to be her parents for an hour or so. A nice plump couple who would cross their arms and nod concernedly while Officer Bergstrom listed the dangers of playing in abandoned cabins. But she didn't have time to set that up.

They drove up Bradley Road and passed some familiar houses. There were lots of tiny winding roads on the hill. They could circle for hours. At Blair Street, Zoe said, "Turn here." Two blocks up she said, "Stop here."

Officer Bergstrom pulled over. She'd taken him right to Mrs. Garmo's house. They got out of the car and headed up the front steps. Officer Bergstrom rang the bell. Zoe's heart pounded wildly as she waited. What would she say to Mrs. Garmo? It wasn't like she was going to pull off a sudden grandmother act.

Rain pattered on the steps. Sometimes Mrs. Garmo took forever coming to the door. Zoe grabbed the railing, a rushing sound filling her ears. Any second now she was going to go off like a bomb. Fly into zillions of pieces, and Mrs. Garmo would have to use the Shop-Vac to clean the mess up.

Now Officer Bergstrom was knocking on the door and ringing the bell impatiently. Zoe drew a breath. "I'll get the key," she said, heading for the hidden stone behind the rosebush.

A minute later she let them in and nearly died of happiness. The house was empty, and there on the wall of the entryway was the photo Mrs. Garmo had taken of Zoe and her poodles a few weeks back. It showed Zoe kneeling down between Jinx and Tiddlywink. Mrs. Garmo had had the picture framed and everything.

"Nobody's here," said Juke.

"Dad planned to get work done on the van today," said Zoe. "And Mom must be at the store." It felt so good to tell the truth.

"When will they be back?" asked Officer Bergstrom.

"I don't know." Zoe smiled and stood beside her photo just in case Officer Bergstrom hadn't noticed it yet.

"Nice poodles," he said.

"Their names are Jinx and Tiddlywink," said Zoe proudly.

"Tiddlywink the poodle," said Juke, finally saying something good for a change.

"Well," said Officer Bergstrom, looking out the window. "I don't have time to wait around." He took off his shades and focused his deep blue eyes on Juke and Zoe. "Promise me two things," he said.

Zoe took a step back. "Sure."

"First, you'll never go near that cabin again."

"Sure," said Juke.

"Okay," said Zoe, feeling the loss of her secret place as soon as she said the word.

"Second," he said, bending lower, "you'll obey all the bike laws. Don't ride at night without a bike light. Wear your bike helmet. And for goodness' sake, get off your bike on that steep hill leading down to the bridge." He said the last words with such vehemence that Zoe knew he was thinking of Julia. Her bike light hadn't been working that night, and she wasn't wearing her helmet. Aliya had told her that much.

"We'll be careful," said Zoe softly.

Back outside they pulled the bikes from the patrol car trunk and parked them at the side of the house. Then, loaded down with sleeping bags, they waved good-bye to Officer Bergstrom as he pulled away from the curb.

"Wow, that was close!" said Juke.

"No kidding."

"Good thinking to come here."

"I wasn't thinking, I was . . . feeling my way along."

Juke shrugged. "So, what do we do now?"

"We'll ditch our stuff under the porch," said Zoe,

"then I'll call Dad's cell phone." They hadn't much time. If Mrs. Garmo was on a walk with the dogs, she was likely to return soon.

Dad was pretty surprised when Zoe phoned. She told him they'd left the cabin and were hanging out at Mrs. Garmo's.

"I didn't know you had to walk the poodles this morning," said Dad.

Zoe toyed with the idea of telling Dad that Mrs. Garmo wasn't at home and decided against it. "The thing is," said Zoe, "we were told to leave the cabin. It's kind of off-limits." Silence on the other end. "Don't worry, we got all the stuff out first. So how's the van?"

"The engine block's cracked. It'll take another day or two before they can replace it. Listen," said Dad, "I'll try to catch up with your mom before she heads back to the cabin. Can you meet us at Winslow Park in about forty minutes?"

"Yeah, sure," said Zoe. She didn't want to tell Dad how hard it was going to be to get down the hill with all their stuff. She could tell by the sound of his voice how worried he was. "Just a minute, Dad." Zoe walked down the hall to the kitchen, where she spotted Juke rummaging through the pantry. "Get outta there, Juke," she said. "That's not our food!"

"What's going on?" asked Dad on the other end of the line.

"Nothing, Dad. See you soon." Zoe pushed the OFF button on Mrs. Garmo's mobile and replaced the phone.

"I didn't eat nothin'," said Juke. "But, look, Zoe! Look at all this food! She probably wouldn't get too mad if I had a couple of crackers or something."

Zoe's stomach ached with hunger. They'd had peanut butter sandwiches for dinner around five thirty last night before they'd gone trick-or-treating. Since then all she'd had was candy. Mrs. Garmo's shelves were crammed with cans and boxes. Terrific crackers and cereals. She even had a can of Cheez Whiz. Juke reached for the crackers, and Zoe grabbed his hand. "Forget it! It's not ours, I said."

Just then they heard the back door slam. Zoe pulled the pantry door shut. Great! Just great! Mrs. Garmo was back from her walk!

21

It was torture to be hungry and be stuck in Mrs. Garmo's pantry with all that food. The box lid was half open, and Zoe could smell cheese crackers in the air the way you could smell buttered popcorn at the movies. She took a deep breath and tried to calm down, but when she heard the sound of Jinx and Tiddlywink's toenails clacking against the kitchen floor, she felt her insides flip like a pancake.

She really could have used Harry Potter's cloak of invisibility right now. If she and Juke slipped it on, they could walk right past Mrs. Garmo and out the back door. The dogs would bark, of course, but Mrs. Garmo would shush them and send them to their doggie pillows. But magic cloaks like that were hard to come by.

One of the poodles sniffed under the door and started barking. "Yes, you've been a very good girl, Tiddly," said Mrs. Garmo. "But quiet down or you won't get your treat!"

Zoe climbed on the little stepping stool in the corner and unscrewed the lightbulb partway. Outside Tiddlywink switched from barking to whining. "She can smell us," whispered Juke.

"Shh."

Tiddlywink scratched on the pantry door. "My goodness, you shouldn't get so worked up over a Milk-Bone, Miss Tiddly! Now go to your pillow and lie down next to Jinx or there'll be no treat today!" She snapped her fingers. "Go on."

Zoe stepped down, grabbed Juke, and shoved him in the corner just before the door swung open. They hid in the corner behind the door as Mrs. Garmo stepped in and pulled on the string. "Darn!" she whispered, peering up at the bulb. "Did I get any bulbs when I went to the store?" she asked herself as she took two Milk-Bones from the box. "I don't think I did," she said before shoving the box back onto the shelf and shutting the door. "Here, girls. Eat up. Now you stay here on your pillows. I'll be right back."

As Mrs. Garmo left the kitchen to look for a new bulb, Zoe grabbed another couple of Milk-Bones and opened the door. Tiddlywink stood up and barked. "Hi, Tiddly," whispered Zoe. "Want another treat?" She tossed Tiddlywink another bone, tossed a second to Jinx, and beat it out the back door with Juke close behind.

Grabbing their bikes, they snuck around to the front porch, where they threw on their backpacks and loaded the sleeping bags onto the handlebars. In their haste to get away, Zoe kicked the jack-o'-lantern over and the candle spilled out.

"Smooth move," said Juke.

"Shut up."

"What's going on out here?" said Mrs. Garmo stepping onto the porch.

"Uh . . . ," said Zoe.

Mrs . Garmo eyed Zoe's sleeping bag. "Just got back from a sleepover," spouted Zoe. "And—"

"And I asked her about your poodles," added Juke.

"Well, come in young man. What's your name?"

"Juke."

"Well, come on in, children." They put their stuff down in the front hall and followed Mrs. Garmo back to the kitchen. "I've been meaning to talk to you anyway, Zoe," said Mrs. Garmo as she took down some glasses and filled them with milk. "I've got a new backyard fence going up next week, and I plan to paint it myself. Would you have time next weekend to help out with that?"

"Sure, I guess," said Zoe.

"I can pay you eight dollars an hour," said Mrs. Garmo.

"Eight bucks an hour?" asked Juke.

"It's worth it," said Mrs. Garmo as she offered Juke some crackers. "I know I can get the fence done in a weekend with Zoe helping out." She passed the cracker plate to Zoe. "So what do you say?"

"Sounds good!" said Zoe. She must have sounded happy because the poodles came right over to the table, wagging their stubby tails in unison.

"Good-bye," called Mrs. Garmo as they left her front yard. "You can come and visit my girls anytime."

Talk about a crazy morning. Here they'd driven to Mrs. Garmo's house with Officer Bergstrom, pretended to live there, hidden in the pantry, unscrewed the light-bulb, and snuck outside only to be invited back in, given milk and crackers, encouraged to play tug-of-war with Jinx and Tiddlywink, and last of all, Zoe was offered a new job.

"Weird," said Juke as they headed down the hill.

"Totally weird," agreed Zoe. "Sort of like the story of Hansel and Gretel. Only we didn't eat the house."

"And Mrs. Garmo's not a witch," said Juke.

"And there weren't any poodles in that story."

"Good thing," said Juke, "or the stepmother would have cooked some poodle stew."

"Don't make me puke!" said Zoe.

They met Mom and Dad at Winslow Park and stood together by an old picnic table. It would be two more days before they'd have their van back, and the cabin was definitely out.

"What about the Salvation Army?" asked Zoe. "I read on the Internet that lots of people can get shelter there."

Dad shook his head. "There's no Salvation Army shelter here in Scout River," he said.

Mom took Dad's hand and gave it a squeeze. "I know you don't want to touch the money we've been saving, Hap."

Dad reached back to adjust the ponytail that was no longer there and ran his hand through his short hair instead. "It'll set us back, Sadie. The cost of the van repairs alone is going to swallow a good chunk of the money."

He watched the gray-brown river flowing past the bridge. A cloud swept overhead, erasing his shadow from the ground. Zoe shivered and stared at the rust on her bike pedal. Anything not to look at her parents leaning against the picnic table, looking hard at Scout River as if the rushing water were going to tell them what to do.

Juke climbed on the table. "I'm hungry."

"No, you're not," said Zoe. "We just ate."

"What would you say to the Starlight Motel?" said Dad.

"I'd love a hot bath," said Mom wistfully.

Zoe frowned. "But we don't have the money to—"

"Why don't you let us worry about that," said Dad.

22

The Starlight was great. The whole family ate popcorn and watched nature shows on TV, and Zoe got to take an hour-long bubble bath. You could build a huge bubble mountain in the tub if you poured enough stuff out of those little free shampoo bottles. Around ten P.M. they bedded down, feeling warm and cozy under the clean covers.

"Who wants a movie of the mind?" asked Dad.

"I do," said Juke.

"I do," said Zoe.

"Screens ready?"

"Ready."

"Picture the ocean on a sunny day," said Dad.

"That's easy," said Juke.

"Shh!" warned Zoe.

"'The Selkie's Treasure,'" said Dad, pitching his voice to a low Irish brogue so that it sounded like Grandpa

Flynn's. "Once long ago a selkie saw a deal of gold on the surface of the sea, and thinking she'd be rich, she came ashore to gather all the coins. . . ."

Zoe fell asleep halfway through the tale, but that didn't matter. She'd heard the selkie story lots of times from Grandpa Flynn before he died and from her Dad in the years after that. Now all the pictures fell into her sleepy eyes, and the selkie came into the human world just as Zoe left it behind for a sea dream.

The next day at school Zoe had an almost-fight with Aliya in the lunchroom, and it was all about houses. Zoe wasn't sure how they'd gotten on the subject, except for the fact that a firefighter had lectured them on fire safety that morning. At the end of the lecture he'd given them an assignment to draw their homes and map out all the escape routes their families could use in case of fire.

"You've always got some reason why I can't come over," said Aliya as she pulled a mushroom off her pizza slice. "One time you said, 'My dad's polishing the hard-wood floors.' Another time you said, 'My mom has a cold and it's catching.' Let's see, what did you tell me last week?" She tugged a second mushroom off the cheese topping. "Oh, yeah, you said, 'My dad's redoing the driveway. Wet cement. So let's go to your house.'" She plucked a black olive from her pizza and ringed it around her pinky finger. "I don't think you're ever going to have me over."

"Oh, I will." Zoe pointed to the abandoned mush-rooms. "Can I have them?"

"Don't change the subject," said Aliya, sweeping her mushrooms onto Zoe's napkin.

Zoe took a bite. "I'm not." The mushrooms were rubbery. Kind of like shredded bicycle tires, only with pizza flavoring.

"So what's the reason this time?" said Aliya.

"Juke's sick."

Aliya flicked her olive onto her tongue. "I saw him at early recess."

"Dentist appointment. After school, I mean. So Mom said—"

Aliya stood up.

"Where are you going?"

"Nowhere."

"Sit down. There's something I want to ask you."

Aliya crossed her arms.

"Please. Just for a minute."

Aliya sat again, waiting. Zoe pushed her lunch sack aside. "It's about the science project."

"I thought we were talking about your house, Zoe."

"I was thinking we could come up with a project together, and we could do some of the experiments over at your house."

"I'm busy."

"We don't have to start today."

Aliya's eyes narrowed on Zoe. "This has happened to me before, you know."

"What? What do you mean?"

Aliya left without answering.

Zoe had her binder open on the small round table at the Starlight Motel.

"How's the homework going?" asked Mom.

"Fine." She tried to concentrate, but Aliya's face kept popping into her head. It was pretty clear that her friendship with Aliya was going downhill. The only way to stop the downward slide was to invite her over. A total cinch if you had a house. Zoe chewed her pencil. So far Aliya was her only friend in Scout River, and she didn't want to lose her. She thought about taking her to Mrs. Garmo's house like she'd done with Officer Bergstrom, then chucked the idea. She couldn't do a rerun of that act for anyone.

She put her pencil to the paper and focused on the assignment. Drawing a fire escape plan was a no-brainer if you had a house to draw. She wrote her name at the top of the page. It would be stupid to draw the motel room they were staying in now, and there was no way on planet Earth she was going to draw their broken-down van.

She pulled out a ruler and began to sketch the outline of 18 Hawk Road. It wasn't like a real drawing with colors and everything. Just a lot of straight lines, so it was pretty safe to do in public. No impossible horses or pink moons for kids to laugh at. Zoe penciled in the upstairs, the downstairs. All the doors and windows in the old two-story house. There would be a prize for the best fire escape plan, and the person who won would get their picture sent to the fire department for its display wall. Not that she expected to win.

Zoe drew arrows to show the escape routes upstairs and down. Below she listed the detached garage as the family meeting place. It was up on the street and far enough away from the house to meet safely in a fire.

The address was more difficult. She couldn't write 18 Hawk Road. There wasn't a Hawk Road in Scout River, so she made up an address that fit the place where they'd been camping out at the end of Cascade Drive. Anyway, it was just a house plan. It wasn't like anyone was going to check out the address.

23

Zoe slammed the van door. "Dibs on the mattress!"

Juke and Zoe both tore off their shoes and went for the foam pad behind the backseat.

"Back off!" yelled Zoe.

"Make me!"

"You're dead!" screamed Zoe. She pushed Juke down on the sleeping platform, grabbed his T-shirt, and twisted.

"Stop it, dog breath!" screamed Juke. "Get offa me now!"

The van door slid open and Mom poked her head in. "Zoe, let go of your brother!"

Zoe rolled off, her heaving chest hot as a fire pit.

"Can you be civil to each other, please?" Mom's face looked haggard, and Zoe noticed dark circles under her eyes. She handed Juke a tissue. "Wipe your nose, son."

"How long are you gonna be?" asked Juke.

"The last load's almost done, then there's the dryer cycle. Why don't you both read or get some homework done."

"Yeah, right," said Zoe.

"Zoe?"

"Okay." She rubbed her pounding temples.

"Good," said Mom and she shut the door. Zoe watched her walk back inside, her thin frame slipping through the half-open door. She turned and grabbed her backpack. "I could have gone to Aliya's after school today instead of being stuck at this stupid Laundromat."

Juke sniffed. "You shouldn't be going there anyway."

"Who says?"

"They're Muslim, right?"

Zoe's hair stuck out on the back of her neck. "So?"

"So Ted Greenway says they should go back to where they came from."

"Who in the heck is Ted Greenway?"

"He's the biggest kid in third grade!"

"He's also the dumbest! Aliya and her family are Americans. This *is* their home. Next time Ted says something like that, tell him to shut up!"

Juke snorted.

"What's so funny?"

"Me telling Ted to shut up. I'd get pounded into hamburger in seconds flat." He blew his nose and looked at his snot. "It's green," he announced. "Wouldn't it be cool if snot glowed in the dark?"

Zoe unzipped her pack.

"When I grow up," said Juke, "I'm gonna invent something you can drink to make your snot glow in the dark."

"I thought you were going to invent cars that fly."

"Yeah, that, too," said Juke.

Zoe reached into her backpack for her book and pulled out her progress report along with it. The stupid piece of paper just wouldn't stay put. She turned her back to Juke and pinched the folded page between sweaty fingers. She'd been at the top of her class back in Tillerman, with big red A's on most of her papers, but that was before. Zoe bit the inside of her cheek as she unfolded the page and scanned the list of incomplete assignments.

Grades were typed beside each subject area. One C, three D's, and two F's. The grades weren't final, but report cards would be out in a few weeks and there wasn't time to make up all the missing work before then.

"What are you looking at?" asked Juke.

"Nothing. Read your book." Juke took out a toy car and rolled it across the mattress.

At the bottom of the page was a line for the parent's signature. Zoe had written *Sadie Flynn* with a fine ballpoint pen. She peered at the slender cursive *S*. The shape had to be just right to fool Ms. Eagle.

🚌

The progress report was safely hidden away by the time Mom opened the van door and pushed the clothes box under the sleeping platform.

"Okay," said Mom, "seat belts."

Zoe beat Juke into the front seat. Mom turned the ignition, and the engine rumbled to a start. The van shook like an old bony dog, and Zoe felt it rattling all through her body.

"You sure they fixed this right?" asked Juke.

"I asked you to buckle up!" snapped Mom.

Zoe watched the Laundromat shrink in the rearview mirror as they pulled out of the parking lot. Mom didn't use to snap at Juke like that, but then, back home in Tillerman she had her beloved garden to chill out in. No garden here. And dirt wasn't something to grow prizewinning roses in. Here it was just something she had to wash out of the clothes.

They stopped at a red light, and Zoe leaned back and closed her eyes. She'd doze off like Sleeping Beauty and wake up a hundred years later with Prince Asif leaning over her. He'd carry her away from the rusty old van and bring her to his exotic castle, where they'd hold a great feast. She'd stuff herself with warm *parathas* swimming in ghee, and in the evening she'd burn her progress report in the stone fireplace. Merlin would wag his tail and sit beside her near the hearth as the progress report turned to ash.

The van turned a corner, and Zoe nearly lost hold of her daydream, but she squeezed her eyelids tighter till bright colors bloomed inside her lids. She'd left something out. Oh, yeah. Mom and Dad would have a special section of her castle to live in. There would be this amazing rose garden just for Mom to lose herself in. And Juke would have a big walled-off playroom down near the dungeon.

24

On Thursday afternoon Zoe biked downtown. They'd been back in the van only three days now, and things were worse than ever. She'd like to kick that stupid van down the side of the cliff into the sea. Watch it burn as it tumbled down the jagged rocks, the way cars did in the movies. Short of that, she had four dollars and fifty cents in her pocket to buy another Mars Meal at Galaxy Burgers.

The rain had stopped hours ago, but the puddles were full. She splashed through on her bike as she pedaled past half-lit houses. Halloween decorations still hung in the windows. Soggy scarecrows sprawled on the front porches. At the far end of town she pulled up at Galaxy Burgers, stepped in line, and put in her order.

Zoe stepped aside and let the guy with the pierced eyebrow order next. She filled out the little blue square Customer Comments sheet while she waited. On the skinny lines she wrote: *Why don't you serve a veggie burger here? You would get a lot of new customers that way, and you could call it the Venus Veggie Burger. I know at least one family who would eat here pretty often if you did that!*

She had to squeeze the last four words up along the side of the little square paper. And she'd covered over the place where you could sign your name, so she wrote *Zoe* at the end of her comment and slipped it into the box. Fat chance the people here would take her up on it, but Mom would be proud of her for trying to shift their attitude.

Zoe took her Mars Meal minus the meat to the corner table. She jammed her straw down into the shake and let the cold sweet chocolate taste fill her head. As soon as she won the Intergalactic Cash Prize, she'd buy back her house. If they got home soon, there might still be a few red leaves hanging on the maple tree in the patio off the sunroom. At nightfall Mom would light the fire in the fireplace. They'd sit in the warm light and watch the flames dance across the wood. Then Zoe would lie down next to Merlin, put her finger in the air, and trace ceiling cracks that were etched like ancient stories written in a secret code.

The song "Fly Me to the Moon" came on the overhead speaker. Zoe extracted the Intergalactic Game Card from her sack and pinched it between her fingers. Her toes curled inside her sneakers. She took a sip of her shake for strength, her heart doing a rock-'n'-roll number in her chest. Right now down in Tillerman kids were out of school and heading home. She'd be one of them soon if this was the right game card. She gripped the card tighter and closed her eyes. *Home*, she thought, the word sounding strange and magical in her mind. A chant a wizard would use to break an evil spell.

Another french fry, then Zoe placed the card on the orange table and began to scratch the silver circles. First word: *You*. Second word: *Have*. Third word: *Won!*

25

The words on the card filled her with white lightning. "I won!" she screamed, leaping up and spilling her fries across the table. A million-dollar win! She'd done it! Zoe raced to the front counter, swinging her coat over her head like a lasso. "Everything! I won everything!" she shouted.

"Hey, cool it," said the girl behind the cash register. "People are trying to eat in here."

"I won!" yelled Zoe, shoving the card in her face. "See!"

"Okay," said the girl. She turned the card over, scratched the back side, and gave it back to Zoe. Zoe read the words on the back: *Free Saturn Shake!* Her ears started ringing like there were a bunch of telephones inside her head.

"You want that now?"

"That's it?" said Zoe. "I mean . . . a milk shake?"

The girl flipped back her brown hair. "That's what the game card says."

"What about the big Intergalactic—"

"There are lots of ways to win," interrupted the manager, stepping up behind the counter and flashing a smile. "If you don't want the shake, you can have a chocolate Galaxy Bar."

Zoe should have looked up and smiled back, but she couldn't move. For a whole minute she'd been a millionaire. She'd had the power to bring everything back. Her home on Hawk Road, her dog, her room, her friends— her whole life. She'd felt so light, she could have flown out the Galaxy Burgers window. Sped past the moon and right up into the stars.

Now the streak of white lightning that had zapped her just a moment before was blinking like a burned-out flashbulb in a cheap camera.

"So, will it be the shake or what?" said the girl.

Zoe dropped the game card in the trash.

Flight canceled.

She walked out the door. Her feet felt like a couple of bricks.

26

Mallory had been watching her all morning. Two blue eyes moved about like searchlights wherever she went. Zoe pretended not to notice, but little trickles of sweat kept running down her neck. Okay, so the fire escape drawings were on the wall for everyone to gawk at. She'd gotten an A on hers, and Mallory had gotten a C. And, yeah, she'd won the blue ribbon for the best fire escape plan. Some of the kids, including Brad and Jamal, were taking their eyes off Mallory and checking Zoe out for once. The attention felt kind of nice, but Mallory wasn't used to sharing the spotlight.

When the recess bell rang, Zoe raced out the door hoping for some relief, but Mallory and her group followed her and Aliya outside and watched their tetherball match like it was some big important game. Between matches Zoe raced to the fountain and downed some water. She could feel Mallory's eyes on her, but she didn't turn around.

A spell wand would come in handy just about now. She could tap the fountain, say a few magic words, and suddenly the tiny clear stream she was sipping would grow into a mighty river. She'd sail across the schoolyard in a beautiful ship, catch a southern breeze right down to California, and moor the boat on the shores of Tillerman. Short of that, she could use her wand to cast a forgetting spell on Mallory. Make her forget about the fire escape plans on the classroom wall.

"Hey," said the boy in line behind her, "you gonna finish drinking sometime this week?"

Zoe stepped away from the fountain for him to drink.

"Yeah, you shouldn't crowd the fountain, zoo girl," said Mallory.

Zoe wiped her wet mouth and tried to press past the crowd gathering near the fountain.

"What's your hurry?" said Mallory.

"We're playing tetherball," said Zoe.

"Looks like your place is taken," said Mallory, waving her hand at Val and Crystal. Val raced across the playground, grabbed the tetherball, and swung it around the pole.

"We'll play something else, then," said Aliya.

"What if I told you I wanted to talk to my servant alone?" said Mallory.

The word *servant* shot ice slivers down Zoe's legs. Aliya crossed her arms. "I don't see any servants."

Mallory pointed to Zoe.

"Come on," said Aliya, taking Zoe by the arm. "Don't mind her."

They veered left, and Mallory stepped in front of them. "Does she vacuum your room when she goes to your house?"

"No. Of course not."

Zoe licked her sweaty upper lip. Where was this vacuum thing heading?

"Just wondering, because my neighbor across the street hires zoo girl's mom to clean her house once a week."

"That's a lie!" said Zoe.

"Hey, I know that ugly green van your parents pick you up in when I see it. And just last week I saw your mom vacuuming Mrs. Leonard's living room from my own bedroom window."

"It wasn't my mom you saw," said Zoe. Of course the lie sounded totally lame. Her body was shaking as she looked at Mallory's freckled face.

"I can prove she's a liar," said Mallory. "You know that fire escape drawing she got the prize for? Well, there's no way she can afford that kind of house. Three bedrooms and a library room upstairs? A sunporch with a piano? Come on."

"It's my home," said Zoe.

"Yeah, right."

"Get out of our way!" said Aliya.

"Maybe the zoo girl lives at the zoo," said Shannon.

"I say she's trailer trash, and she's too ashamed to admit it," said Mallory.

"Smells like trailer trash to me," said Kelly.

"I'd know that stink anywhere," said Shannon.

Aliya stepped between Zoe and Mallory. "She doesn't live in the mobile home park."

"Yeah? How do you know?" said Mallory. "Ever been to her house?"

Aliya's eyes went wide. "No. I haven't, but—"

"I thought you were friends," said Mallory.

"We are."

"And she's never had you to her house?" Mallory turned to Kelly. "See?" said Mallory. "I told you."

Kelly licked her lips. "We should tell Ms. Eagle that big two-story house she drew for the fire escape assignment is all a lie."

"Yeah," said Shannon. "Zoe's house plan should be taken off the wall. She should give that ribbon back!"

Ms. Eagle led her class to the gym for an afternoon assembly, so Shannon didn't get her chance to rat on Zoe. During the play titled *Healthy Habits*, as little kids danced around the stage in giant carrot and cabbage costumes, Zoe eyed the wall clock, waiting for her moment. They were heading into a four-day weekend. All she had to do was get out fast.

When the last bell rang, she beat it back to class and flew out the door with her backpack. She was putting on her bike helmet when Aliya came up the walk.

"I can't come over today," said Zoe.

"So?" said Aliya. "I'm busy myself. In fact, my weekend is full." Zoe tightened her helmet strap and adjusted her backpack.

"If you had invited me to your house sometime," said Aliya, "I could have told Mallory off, but I couldn't defend you, Zoe. I had nothing to say." She looked at Zoe accusingly then, waiting for an answer. Zoe fiddled with her rusty bike lock.

"It's because I'm Muslim, isn't it?" said Aliya.

"What?" said Zoe. "What does that have to do with it?"

"Someone in your family doesn't want a Muslim girl coming to their house."

"No way. That's not a problem."

"It's happened to me before, Zoe. A good friend, I thought. But then I was never invited over. She never—"

"I told you, that's not the problem!"

"Then what is it? Why haven't you ever asked me to your house?" Zoe felt Aliya's soft brown eyes move across her slowly as she waited for her answer. The silence lasted only seconds, but it might as well have been a hundred years. Zoe bit the inside of her cheek. She looked down to pull the lock chain through the rack, and Aliya left her there.

Still stooping by the rack, Zoe watched her only friend in Scout River go down the cracked sidewalk and turn the corner. At first everything was quiet, like hunks of cotton had been stuffed into Zoe's ears. Then she leaped up and kicked her tire hard. Her toe cramped with pain as all the bikes on the rack went crashing down.

The sound they made wasn't loud enough. She wanted an explosion. She wanted tumbling walls and smoke and broken glass. She wanted the wreckage she was feeling inside to show.

27

The sign at the ticket counter read
BE RIGHT BACK. Zoe jammed her hands in her coat pockets
and waited on the bus station bench. The man across from
her stared at the ceiling while he ran his battery-oper-
ated shaver across his chin. There was no way she was
going to sit next to *him* on the bus. It was a long ride to
California. Too long to spend next to a guy who shaved in
public.

Her plan had gone pretty smoothly so far. Mom and
Dad thought she was spending the four-day weekend at
Aliya's to work on their science project. That would work
out okay as long as they didn't try to call Aliya's house.
She didn't think they would. They'd been happy to drop
her and her stuff off this morning at the top of the
Faruquis' long driveway. And when they pulled away,
she'd ducked behind a bush to wait awhile before taking
a shortcut down the hill to the bus station.

Juke was spending part of the weekend with his friend Gabe at the trailer park. That meant Mom and Dad would have the van to themselves for a few days. They wouldn't expect to hear from her until Monday, and by then she'd be long gone.

An old lady in a baggy orange dress sat down beside Mr. Public Shave. She unrolled some toilet paper and blew her nose. Zoe bit her nail and looked the other way. Maybe the bus wouldn't be too full and she could find a seat by herself. The clock on the wall read ten A.M. More and more people were filing into the station and hanging around the ticket counter.

Zoe leaned back on the hard bench. The bus station smelled like stale cigarettes with a little rotten fruit on the side. Someone had tried to eliminate the smells with pine cleaner, but it hadn't worked too well. A fat lady wearing a SAVE THE ANIMALS T-shirt scooted onto the bench next to her. Her long brown hair was in two slender braids with beads and pink feathers at the ends.

"Happy Friday," said the lady, extending her hand over her grocery bag. "The name's Georgia." Her dark blue eyes sparkled.

"I'm Zoe."

Georgia smiled. "So where are you heading?"

"San Francisco," said Zoe.

"Me too."

"I'm going to visit my grandmother for the weekend."

"All by yourself?"

"I've done it lots of times," said Zoe. It was true, she'd bused to her grandma's place twice before, but not from so far away, and both times Grandma Nell had met her at the station.

"I work at Pet Pals," said Georgia. "You ever been there?"

"I've seen the kittens in the window."

"Cute, aren't they?" Georgia sighed happily. The man across from them stood up and paced back and forth. "Did you know there are cat people and dog people? I can always tell within two minutes of meeting someone," Georgia said.

Zoe tugged on her torn fingernail. "Oh, yeah? What am I, then?"

Georgia pursed her lips, then nodded once. "Dog person."

"Big dog or little?"

"Oh, big, I'd say. You like collies, Labs, golden retrievers."

Zoe shivered.

"What's the dog's name?" asked Georgia.

"Merlin," said Zoe. "How did you know?"

"I told you, I can always tell."

The crowd moved forward.

"She's back," said Georgia. They both grabbed their stuff and got into the line forming at the ticket counter.

"Sure is hot in here," said Georgia.

"Yeah," said Zoe, only she thought it was kind of cold herself. When they reached the counter, Georgia put her grocery sack on the floor next to her suitcase and bought her bus ticket.

"I've got a suitcase to check," said Georgia. She hefted the bulging case onto the low counter next to the ticket stand.

"Next," said the lady behind the glass window.

Georgia carried her shopping bag across the station to the ticket holders' line.

"One for San Francisco," said Zoe.

"Traveling alone?" asked the lady behind the counter. Her painted eyebrow tilted upward.

"I'm with her," said Zoe, pointing to Georgia with her thumb. "My aunt Georgia's taking me to see the grandparents."

She waved at Georgia. Georgia waved back, then pointed next to her to show she was saving Zoe a place in line.

"That'll be forty dollars." The woman at the counter fiddled with her hoop earring as Zoe pulled out her fence-painting money and put three ten-dollar bills and two fivers on the counter.

"Bags to check?" she asked.

"No," said Zoe, grabbing her backpack.

People had already started boarding by the time Zoe got outside. She climbed onto the bus and looked for Georgia. Mr. Public Shave was already seated in the second row. Behind him sat a lady knitting a Christmas sweater. Farther up the aisle the toilet-paper lady was struggling with her bags. Two middle-aged twin sisters stood behind her, coaching her on where to stash her stuff. The twins were dressed in matching yellow pantsuits with bright orange scarves. It was like being stuck behind a couple of parade floats. Zoe couldn't even see around them.

At last the line moved forward, and more people took their seats. Near the back of the bus she spotted Georgia. Zoe settled into her seat and swung her backpack onto her lap.

"Made it," she said.

"Welcome to the back of the bus," said Georgia.

Zoe tightened the rope across her sleeping bag. The peanut butter sandwich near the top of the pack was probably squashed flat by now. Well, food was food, it didn't have to look good to be good. The rest of the stuff she'd jammed in her pack would keep her going for a while. Some books, a change of clothes, hairbrush, and toothbrush. She'd wanted to pack more, but you couldn't very well lug a ton of stuff over to a friend's house without causing some suspicion.

The bus rumbled to a start and turned onto Miller Avenue.

"So, where do you call home here in Scout River?" asked Georgia.

Zoe blinked. "What?"

"Where do you live?"

"Oh, uh, up in the hills."

"Great place, Scout River," said Georgia. "I wouldn't be leaving if I wasn't on a big-sister rescue mission."

Zoe wasn't sure what Georgia meant by a "big-sister rescue mission," but she decided not to ask. It might be personal.

The light changed and the bus lurched forward. Georgia pulled a grapefruit out of her sack. "Grapefruit fast," she said. "I'm gonna lose five pounds on this trip."

A little white spray of juice spurted out of the rind as Georgia peeled her grapefruit. Zoe leaned her head against the window and thought about the real answer to Georgia's question: *Where do you call home here in Scout River?* The answer was no place. That's why she was leaving.

By the time they'd reached the Oregon border, Georgia had told Zoe about her crazy little sister, Evie, who was always getting into trouble. "So she called me again a couple of nights back, and here I am on the bus to S.F. to help her out of another stupid mess," said Georgia. "It's become kind of a yearly ritual."

"What happened this time?" asked Zoe.

"Oh, her boyfriend, Clueless Hugh, got arrested for . . ." She cleared her throat. "It's complicated."

"Complicated doesn't scare me," said Zoe.

"Yeah, well, let's just say *some* grown-ups need to go back to kindergarten and learn a few basic rules."

"I know some grown-ups like that," said Zoe. "My kindergarten teacher, Mrs. Rand, used to say, 'People aren't for punching.'"

"People aren't for punching. That's a good one."

Georgia finished peeling another grapefruit. "Sure you don't want a bite?" Zoe shrugged and took a section. You could eat almost anything if you were hungry enough.

Eleven hours, nine grapefruits, and six diet sodas later, they hit the San Francisco city limits. It was after ten P.M. when the bus pulled into the depot. Georgia picked a few stray grapefruit rinds off the floor. "Is your grandma meeting you at the bus?"

"Inside the station," said Zoe, peering out the window. The street was well lit, but there weren't many people out walking by the depot. She'd hoped the bus wouldn't reach San Francisco until morning. No such luck. Before disembarking, Georgia pulled a pink feather from one of her braids and handed it to Zoe. "Nice getting to know you, kid," she said.

"Good luck with Clueless Hugh," said Zoe.

Georgia shrugged. "Yeah, thanks."

Zoe stepped into the bus station and checked out the schedules. Her transfer bus wouldn't leave until the next morning. She knew she couldn't sit on the bench all night without some grown-up asking her a bunch of questions. Besides, there was a guy sitting in the corner with tattoos all over his arms, and he kept looking her way. She headed for the rest room, used the bathroom, washed her face, and checked herself out in the mirror. Her short brown hair was sticking out, her brown eyes looked even bigger than usual, and her pale face was all splotchy. She brushed her hair and teeth. It didn't alter her appearance a whole lot, but it was good to get that grapefruit taste out of her mouth.

Hearing footsteps just outside the door sent Zoe racing into the nearest stall. The lady with the shiny black boots took way too long in front of the mirror. Probably putting on her makeup. Zoe sat on the toilet seat and waited. After a while she propped her backpack on the toilet-paper dispenser, leaned her head against her sleeping bag, and fell asleep.

Around six in the morning Zoe was awakened by the bus departure announcement blasting over the loudspeaker. She stood up and felt a wet spot on her bottom. Great! She'd fallen partway into the toilet! She did a quick change, held her wet jeans under the hand dryer, then beat it out of the rest room fast, just managing to buy her ticket, race up the steps, and find a seat near the back of the bus.

The driver moved from stop to stop through the downtown streets, and Zoe had to share her seat all the way through the business district. But the thin old man who smelled of arthritis cream got off at the last stop before the driver merged into the thick lines of traffic heading out of the city.

Now with her seat to herself again, Zoe stared out the window as they crossed the Golden Gate Bridge. The water of San Francisco Bay sparkled golden in the morning sun. Something about the dancing light reminded her of "The Selkie's Treasure." She knew the words by heart, and putting her forehead against the cool window, she could almost hear her dad's voice tell the story in her head.

Once long ago a selkie saw a deal of gold on the surface of the sea, and thinking she'd be rich, she came ashore to gather all the coins. There she shed her black sealskin and looked for all the world like a beautiful young girl. She lay her selkie skin on a rock while she searched for the treasure. But no sooner had she taken it off than a man spied her on the shore and fell at once in love with her. Hoping to keep her all to himself, he stole her skin and hid it from her.

Now, a selkie cannot return to the sea without her skin, and so she was caught in the wrong world and doomed to live on the land as an ordinary girl. She married the man, but the poor girl was never truly happy. Then one day after many years had passed, she found her selkie skin hidden in a treasure box high up in the man's attic. As soon as she touched her skin, she remembered her home in the sea, and though she loved the man, she knew the land was not her place. So she slipped on her shining black skin and swam back out into the ocean. And there the selkie found her riches at last, which weren't the gold of this world after all, but only the home she'd left behind.

28

The bus followed the contour of the coast from small town to small town. Zoe had been on this route before, and it always seemed to take forever. Somewhere along the way they lost the sun in the evergreens, and now the driver was going even slower to navigate the morning mist. At last the bus pulled up at the Tillerman depot and let out a gassy hiss. Zoe stepped onto the sidewalk. Morning fog covered everything in sight, as if Tillerman were some secret undersea kingdom. She tightened her backpack straps and headed up the sidewalk, stepping happily between the grassy cracks.

The cowbell on the door of O'Shea's Bakery gave a loud clang. Mr. O'Shea peered over his reading glasses. "Well, hello, Zoe."

"Hey, Mr. O'Shea." Zoe checked out the baskets of cookies, bear claws, and fresh doughnuts in the case. Mr.

O'Shea put down his morning paper. "What's your pleasure?"

"Glazed doughnut, please," said Zoe.

Mr. O'Shea slipped a fat gleaming doughnut into a small white bag and added a napkin. "Say hello to your mother," he said as Zoe handed over her money.

"I will." Zoe smiled as she left the shop. Mr. O'Shea thought they still lived in Tillerman. They'd only gone to the bakery every couple of months to get a special treat, so how would he know they'd moved? It wasn't like there was some big announcement in the newspaper every time a family moved away.

Mr. O'Shea's mistake made her feel good, as if she'd found some secret door back into the past. Like this was one of those special Saturday mornings when Mom had let her walk downtown to buy a doughnut. All she had to do now was walk home, and everything would be just the way it had always been.

The doughnut was still warm and tasted light as a cloud. She took a second bite, licked the glaze as she passed Pet Parade on Garber Avenue, then forced herself to drop the doughnut back into the sack for later. She stood a moment on the corner and looked around. What a perfect town. Tillerman had everything. The best thrift store, the nicest pet shop, the most beautiful stone church with real stained-glass windows, the friendliest school, and the sweetest bakery. They'd been nuts to leave!

Her mood dipped a little as she passed the empty

storefront where Tillerman Hardware used to be, but it lifted again as she left the town center for a neighborhood street. A friendly bassett hound came out of his yard to sniff her jeans and say hello. She gave him a pat and scratched him behind an ear. Smoke puffed from the chimneys and drifted above the tall redwoods. Zoe closed her eyes and walked awhile. It would be fun to see if she could make it all the way home without opening her eyes once. She could probably do it if it weren't for the swollen lines of tar that scarred the old street. Halfway home she stopped to watch Chris Tucker's little brothers playing on the seesaw in their front yard.

"Hey, Isaac! Hey, Matthew!" she called. Isaac got off the seesaw and hurled a dirt clod at her. He missed her by a mile, but then, he was only four. Up the road she turned onto the path and climbed the dirt steps. Now her heart was really pounding. Any minute she'd see the back side of her house. She'd be face-to-face with her bedroom window!

She hiked up the switchback trail past ivy, ferns, poison oak, and little stink plants until she was standing under her bedroom window. The glass was dark. Jessica Jacobs was probably still asleep. It was Saturday morning, after all. The best time to curl up under the soft covers and dream. Zoe took a breath. Okay, the furniture was going to be different. They may have stuck Jessica's bed against the wrong wall. Jessica's "pretty girl" toys would be all over the place. Zoe readied herself for what she might see. *Okay, now!* Zoe grabbed the sill and pulled herself up to look inside.

The shock of what she saw through the glass made her drop back down to the path. She sucked in a couple of breaths and pulled herself up a second time to view the remains of what had once been her room. Naked two-by-fours were nailed into the floor and ceiling. Hunks of new white wallboard leaned against the back wall. There was only one wall still covered in her poppy wallpaper. Everything else was stripped raw. In the center of the room was a worktable covered in plastic. Her room! They'd completely destroyed her room! The Jacobses had wiped out one whole wall. Worst of all, her closet, her dreamroom, was completely gone!

She let herself drop again and stumbled around the side of the house to a pile of demolished wall near the garbage cans. Her old closet door rested on top of the pile. Zoe sat and ran her finger along three crayoned letters—Z O E—at the base of the door. You couldn't! You couldn't just tear someone's life apart like that and throw it in the garbage heap! You couldn't demolish someone's bedroom! Rip down their wallpaper! Smash their walls! And throw away their dreamroom door like it was nothing more than a useless hunk of rotten wood!

29

Zoe lay on her old closet door as the sunlight ate through the morning fog. She wished the clear yellow light would do the same job with her head. She'd come home to think, to get her life back, but the whole thing had backfired. She sat up, wiped her sweaty palms on her jeans, and tried to swallow down the fear that was rising up the back of her throat. What now?

Ferns left cold dew prints on her jeans as she headed for Kellen's house. She'd planned to stay undercover in Tillerman, at least at first, but Kellen could keep a secret. They'd been best friends since they were four years old. Something about swimming naked in a blow-up wading pool and dumping buckets of cold water over a kid's head on the first day you meet seals a friendship up pretty tight.

Laughter came from just ahead. Kellen must be playing on the back deck with her little sister. Zoe was trying to figure out a way to get her away from her kid sister when she heard Kellen giggling out, "Stop it, Jessica."

Zoe froze.

"This is how Mrs. Gonzega walks," said Jessica, spreading her feet out like a duck and waddling across the deck.

Kellen grabbed her belly and laughed. "No more!" she groaned. "I'm gonna laugh myself sick."

Jessica turned around to waddle back across the deck, and Zoe ducked behind a blackberry bush. Suddenly Jessica stopped and pivoted. "Hey, is somebody out there?"

Zoe held her breath, not moving an inch, as Jessica leaned over the rail. "Mandy, if you're spying on us again, you little snitch, I'm going to steal all your troll dolls and hide them where you'll never find them again!"

"Hey, it's nothing," said Kellen, joining Jessica at the rail. "Probably just a squirrel."

"A squirrel, huh? More like a rat."

Kellen had promised never to make friends with Jessica Jacobs, yet here they were on the morning side of what must have been a sleepover. Zoe studied the parts of Kellen's face she could make out through the blackberry leaves. Kellen didn't look like a traitor, but then, what did traitors look like? The kitchen window above the deck flew open, and Kellen's mom poked her head out. "Anyone for pancakes?" The girls raced up the steps and slammed the back door.

🚌

That night, wrapped in her sleeping bag in the storage room above the garage, Zoe replayed the day in her head. Okay, the doughnut had been good, but after that everything had gone crazy, from finding her demolished bedroom to discovering Jessica Jacobs on Kellen's deck. She'd been ready to check out the new friend, Carla, Kellen had mentioned in her letter, but Jessica? It was total betrayal. As soon as Kellen's back door slammed, Zoe had darted back through the woods, raced down the trail to Thompson Road, and walked to town. She'd planned to take the bus over to Calloway to visit Merlin, but only two buses went to Calloway each day, and the afternoon run didn't leave Tillerman till five P.M. So she scrapped that plan and spent the rest of the day walking around town like some crazed ghost looking for a way back into the world.

Hunger finally drove her to the market, where she bought supplies. When the afternoon showers hit, she was driven to find some kind of shelter, so she circled back home. The second good thing that happened (after the glazed doughnut) was finding the door to the storage room above the garage unlocked.

Zoe looked at her watch. Nine o'clock. She turned over, keeping her flashlight close to the floor so no one in the house below would see light coming from the storage-room window. She had to come up with a plan. Some way to get rid of the Jacobses. An idea started to form in the back of her mind as she scrunched down in her sleeping bag. Rain smacked against the glass, and the wind set the redwoods talking. Zoe listened in, wondering what they were saying to one another.

Some kid hiding out in the garage below. Pass it on. Wait, no, they wouldn't say that; they'd known Zoe for years. She listened again.

Zoe's home, they whispered to one another. *Zoe's home.*

30

Zoe finished the Pop-Tart, brushed the crumbs off her sleeping bag, and yawned. She hadn't slept very well last night, so it hadn't helped to be awakened at five thirty by a heavy clunking sound as Mr. Jacobs loaded his golf clubs into his Blazer. What kind of nut hit the road at five thirty on a Sunday morning? She'd fallen into a kind of half sleep after he sped down the road but couldn't get back into her dreams.

Later that morning Zoe watched Mrs. Jacobs leave for church with Jessica and Mandy. As soon as their red minivan turned the corner, Zoe broke free from her hideout, raced for the garden hose, and cranked the spigot. The cool hose water tasted dusty and filled her nose with summer smells. She closed her eyes and drank in more, her head filling with images of long days pitching baseballs, climbing trees, and riding bikes till the sun was way gone and stars were packed out in the heavens.

Zoe filled her empty OJ bottle to the brim and set it by the steps. Okay, she shouldn't go in. Trespassing was a bad idea. But she had to go to the bathroom bad. She tried the front door, and of course it was locked. The kitchen door was next. Locked too. She circled around the back of the house, checking the windows. No go. Then back to the front door again. Her bladder felt like a gorged water balloon. She stepped into the damp dirt behind the rosebush and pushed against the living-room window. It shuddered and slid aside. Presto! She was in! Zoe sped through the living room feeling about as smart as Goldilocks (dumb kid if there ever was one) and tore into the master bathroom.

Wow! What a change! The problem toilet Mom used to spend hours plunging and snaking was gone. The new one flushed without a gurgle. Zoe held her hands under the running water. The new faucet sang. Man, Mom would love the master bathroom now. She could throw the plunger down the never-never hole and lounge around in her new bathroom like a rich lady. Mom could spend her time worrying about stupid little things like chipped fingernails and how to do her hair.

Zoe dried her hands and did a quick tour of the upstairs. Fresh cream-colored paint on all the walls. New furniture everywhere. She closed the living-room window and stood in the patch of sunlight. On weekend mornings she'd come to this window to catch the sun. The old glass broke the light into wave patterns that crossed the hardwood floor to light up the Persian rug.

Now the glass was painting warm white waves across her legs and chest. She'd stay there longer if she could in the silence and the light, but she knew she could be seen from the road above, so she left the window, skirted the pink couch, and peeked into the sunroom.

The ancient piano used to sit out there collecting dust; now the sunroom was crammed with Jessica's and Mandy's stuff, doubling as a bedroom while the downstairs was being gutted. A fat orange tabby trotted in and rubbed against her leg.

"Hey, kitty," said Zoe. She reached down and ran her hand along his soft fur. Georgia was wrong about dog people and cat people. Sometimes she could be a cat person, too. The tabby circled her legs again, lifted his tail, and darted from the room.

Back in the living room Zoe searched for the cat, but he was hiding somewhere. She recrossed the light green area rug, which would have been "Don't Walk" perfect if some idiot hadn't left muddy prints on it. Zoe stopped to check out her sneakers and discovered she was the idiot. Five minutes later she was kneeling barefoot, trying to wash the prints off the area rug with a damp paper towel. The harder she scrubbed, the more the prints clung to the rug, turning into light brown smears that wouldn't go away.

The big stuffed chair was hard to move, but after some pushing on top and pulling on bottom, she managed to tug it over the stain. She should get out now before anyone came home and noticed the change. But she couldn't, not yet, not with her old bedroom just beneath her. Zoe grabbed her shoes and headed for the steps. She was willing to risk getting caught if it meant she could hang out in her room awhile.

In the dark downstairs hall she pushed the door open and stepped inside. The windows hadn't changed and the same redwoods whispered outside her window, but the rest of the room was stripped naked. She'd been ready for that; she already knew a wall was missing and her dreamroom was gone, but she wasn't prepared to see all her poppy wallpaper stripped from the wall. Just yesterday it had covered the wall to the left of her window, and seeing the poppies had given her some comfort. Something of her life would be left in the room. But they'd taken even that.

In the corner of the ceiling she spied her almost elephant. "Do you remember?" she whispered. Outside the wind-washed trees bowed and the elephant's trunk seemed to move in the shadows. She tore a small corner off the wallpaper piled on the floor, and put it in her pocket, then, standing in the middle of her floor, she closed her eyes and puzzled her room back together in her mind piece by piece. With her eyes shut, it was easy to see her bed, dresser, and desk piled up with books. She could see a field of poppies along the wall and her dreamroom door across from that. Her bed was made up with her star quilt on top, and all her stuffed animals were dozing in the morning light falling through her window. She breathed in the faint smell of home, something the Jacobses could never scrub away or strip from the walls or suck up in their vacuum cleaners. It was an old-house smell, and it was full of Flynn magic.

"You're changed and broken and ugly," whispered Zoe. "But I'll take you back if you'll take me back." She put out her arms and spun slowly round and round just to feel the dizzy. White wallboard dust on the floor made a pattern of bare footprints like strange new dance steps as she circled. Nothing else moved. Behind her eyelids everything spun white.

The sudden slam of the upstairs door upset Zoe's spin. She banged against the worktable, grabbed the plastic tarp, and listened to the heavy steps. Mr. Jacobs was back from his golf game. She should have thought of that. He'd left home so early!

Only two doors out, and they were both upstairs. She listened to the steps above as Mr. Jacobs crossed over to the kitchen. The pipes in the walls whispered as he ran the water.

Zoe reached for her shoes and spotted her white dust prints. Talk about leaving evidence behind! Now she heard the sound of footsteps on the landing above. Jeez, he was heading down the stairs! Zoe waddled backward, erasing her prints with her bare feet as she stepped her way into her old bathroom. She climbed onto the toilet seat and was halfway out her little bathroom window when Mr. Jacobs entered her room.

Zoe pressed herself the rest of the way though the tiny window and raced for the woods with the tabby at her heels. Down the path she dove behind a blackberry bush and waited. Seconds later Mr. Jacobs poked his head out the open bathroom window. "Stupid carpenters!" he said.

The cat abandoned the blackberry bush and leaped onto the woodpile. Zoe kept her head down low in case the tabby made a sudden move and gave her away.

"Skittle!" called Mr. Jacobs. "Come back inside." Zoe held her breath and gripped her knees. Skittle licked his paw and began to wash his face.

"Come on, boy, " called Mr. Jacobs. Skittle flicked his tail, then jumped off the woodpile and climbed onto the windowsill. "Good boy," said Mr. Jacobs. "We've got a bone to pick with those carpenters, don't we, Mr. S.?"

Behind the bush Zoe rocked on her heels, waiting for him to close the window before she exhaled. She was glad Mr. Jacobs blamed the carpenters for the open window. They deserved it for tearing up her room. With any luck, they'd be blamed for the muddy prints on the green rug too.

Zoe slipped her sneakers on and took the path down to the street below. She'd come up with a way to get rid of the Jacobses last night, but she needed certain supplies to pull it off.

Mrs. Weanbaum was wiping down the front counter at Pet Parade. "Hi, Zoe," she said. "Haven't seen you for a while now. How's Merlin?"

"Oh, he's good, I guess."

Mrs. Weanbaum folded her cleaning rag and frowned.

"I mean, he's real good," corrected Zoe. The store smelled like dog food on cat food on hamster shavings. Not a great morning smell. She strolled over to the shelves and scanned the cages. "How much for a couple of rats?" she asked.

"You're in luck today. We've got some young ones ready to go."

"I want grown-up rats." Zoe peered into a cage. A big white rat glanced back at her and wiggled his nose.

"Oh, well, they run about five dollars a piece, dear. Will you be needing a cage?"

"Uh," said Zoe. "Just a sec." She reached into her pocket and counted her money. She had exactly four dollars and six cents left. The bus ride down had been expensive. Then the transfer to the local bus. Then she'd bought some food yesterday. She dug deeper in her jeans pockets and came out with another dime.

"How many do you want?"

Zoe looked over at Mrs. Weanbaum. "Uh, I was just thinking about it."

"Well, rats make pretty cute little pets," said Mrs. Weanbaum.

"Oh, they're not for me," said Zoe. "They're kind of a present."

Mrs. Weanbaum's mouth struggled somewhere between a grin and a frown before landing on a smile. She gave Zoe a free Milk-Bone. "Say hello to Merlin for me."

"Yeah, okay."

Zoe wandered over to Fletcher Park for some think time. Last night the rat idea had seemed like a perfect plan. All she had to do was set a few rats loose in the house, and the Jacobses would freak out. Rat infestation! They'd abandon 18 Hawk Road and go in search of another house. A perfect rodent-free house in some faraway town. Preferably across the country. But here in the park, with the wakeful wind at her back, the plan seemed dumb. One of those midnight ideas that bottom out in the light of day.

She watched the little kids play on the jungle gym. She didn't see anyone she knew, which was good because she was supposed to be undercover, but it also made her feel weird, like the whole town had forgotten her. She was some nobody hanging around in their park.

Zoe sat on a swing in the shade of a giant redwood. It wasn't like she was missing life in the van, but she had a dull ache at the back of her neck. Missing Mom. Missing Dad. She thought about calling Dad's cell phone, but they thought she was hanging out at Aliya's. They'd go ballistic if she told them where she was. And, anyway, she couldn't explain what she'd done.

That night in her hideout above the garage Zoe reached the end of *The Wonderful Wizard of Oz* for the fifth time. She'd practically memorized the book by now, but that didn't matter. She smoothed the lump out of the shirt she was using for a pillow and stared at the fat spider on the ceiling. When Dorothy was tired of Oz, she clicked her magic slippers three times. That's all she had to do to head back to Kansas and get back everything she'd lost. But what was a person supposed to do when her home was held hostage by strangers?

31

By ten o'clock Sunday night the ache in her neck had shifted down into her chest. She was thinking about the last time Mom brushed her hair, humming the song "Shenandoah" as she touched the top of Zoe's head and slipped the brush through. Her touch was always so light. Zoe's head was suddenly lonely for that feeling. Her ears were lonely too. Missing the sound of Dad's voice. "Who wants a movie of the mind?" he'd ask, and right now she'd say, "I do!" Dad wouldn't have to tell "The Selkie's Treasure" this time. He could tell Juke's favorite pirate tale, "Barnacle Jack." She would even listen to his story about Everest all the way through without interrupting if she were with him now.

Zoe turned over in her sleeping bag. Dad had tried to tell her the Everest story one night last week when they were at the campsite. It was raining pretty hard, but he was outside cooking up some weird packaged stew he'd gotten cheap from Henry's Camping Supply.

"You know, the guys who go up Everest eat this stew!" he'd said.

Zoe hadn't answered. She just held the umbrella over his head so he could cook in the rain without getting soaked. Mom and Juke waited for dinner in the van. She could hear Juke blasting some planet to smithereens with his intergalactic ray gun. "Zeeuu! Pow!"

Dad shifted position by the camp stove. "I heard this amazing story of a sixty-four-year-old guy who took on the challenge of hiking up Everest, and he—"

"What about girls?"

"Huh?"

"Haven't any girls climbed Everest?"

"Sure, Zoe."

The stew had come to a boil right then, so Dad had to grab the pot holder. She'd cut him off on purpose that night. He'd been trying to cheer her up, and she hadn't let him. She rubbed her temples with the flat of her palms. She could have used some cheering up now.

The moon crossed the sky, leaving the window behind, and Zoe lay awake hour after hour. Before dawn she gave up on the whole sleeping proposition and walked to town. Everything was closed and quiet, like the town itself was dreaming under a blanket of fog. She used the bathroom at the gas station, got a couple of snack packages from the vending machine, and headed back to her hideout to get warm.

The kids in Scout River had a four-day weekend, but not so in Tillerman. Around eight A.M. Jessica left for school dressed in her perfect new jeans with her perfect blond hair pulled back in a perfect gold clip. Later that morning Zoe ate through her raisin supply and wasted some time spying on Jessica's little sister, Mandy, also blond with red apple cheeks. Mandy played in the dirt beside the kitchen steps trying to construct a house for her trolls. She'd tried the same house plan twice, first piling up a big dirt hill and decorating it with leaves, then digging a nice deep tunnel. The first two houses had collapsed, but Mandy hadn't given up. Something about her bullheadedness reminded Zoe of herself as a little kid. Mandy was hard at work on her third house now, lying on her tummy, digging a troll tunnel deeper and deeper into the hill.

Zoe watched Mandy's arm disappear into the dirt hole. Only a few seconds to go now and *boom!* The troll house collapsed again. Zoe laughed out loud, then covered her mouth and ducked behind the curtain. Mandy looked up from her dirt pile and spotted her. At least it looked like she'd spotted her. Zoe wasn't sure until Mandy ran inside and emerged a minute later towing her mom up the garden path.

They were already too near the garage for Zoe to get away down the side steps, so she raced to the back window. Juke's secret way in. But as soon as she saw the slender redwood branch reaching out to the sill, she knew she couldn't risk it.

Now Mandy and her mom were starting up the garage stairway. Zoe darted across the room, grabbed her stuff, and hauled it behind a tall stack of boxes stored in the corner.

". . . just a shadow or something, Mandy," Mrs. Jacobs was saying as she opened the door.

"Nope," said Mandy. "I saw her."

Mrs. Jacobs started to search the room. "Ugh," she said. "Look at these cobwebs."

"She was spying on me through the window," said Mandy. "And she was ugly with me."

"You mean she wasn't nice-looking?" said Mrs. Jacobs, peering behind some boxes across the room from Zoe.

"No. She was ugly with me."

Zoe slid deeper into the dark as Mrs. Jacobs stepped closer and checked out another stack.

"Hmm," she said, opening the top box. "I told Ben I was missing those baking pans. He said he'd checked all these boxes up here. But, look! Here they are!"

"And her hair was dirty dark."

Mrs. Jacobs pulled out a baking sheet. "You can't tell if someone's hair is dirty from that far away, honey." Mrs. Jacobs pulled the box to the floor. Zoe curled up into a ball and wedged herself deeper into the corner.

"Not dirty smelly. Just the color dirty."

"There's no such thing as the color dirty," said Mrs. Jacobs. "Now I can bake some chocolate-chip cookies," she said to herself, holding up the pan.

"I've seen it in my crayon box," said Mandy.

Mrs. Jacobs stood up. Zoe's heart thumped in her ears.

"Come on, honey, let's go."

"What about the bad spy?"

"Probably just a bad dream."

"I wasn't sleeping!"

Mrs. Jacobs hauled the box to the door. "Another one of your imaginary friends, then, honey. Next time you see her, invite her to lunch. And if her hair is the color dirty like you say, we can wash it for her." Zoe watched from behind the boxes as they slipped outside. "And speaking of washing hair," said Mrs. Jacobs, "it's bath time. You want to look nice for kindergarten this afternoon."

"No bath," said Mandy.

"Sorry, it's Bubble Magic time for you." Mrs. Jacobs shut the door, and they were gone.

Zoe uncoiled slowly in the corner and rubbed away the cramp in her leg. A fly stared down at her from the box above. A thousand eyes all giving her the once-over, a bad spy girl with hair that was the color dirty.

By eleven o'clock the carpenters had been sawing wood beside the house for two hours. The loud whiz rang in Zoe's ears and scrambled her insides. Her sleepless night had finally caught up with her, and she was hoping to catch a nap, but the saw was jamming too much sound into her ears for that. Zoe flipped her book open to a drawing of the Cowardly Lion. He was all decked out with a big bow on his tail. She was just tracing his mane with her finger when the door flew open and Mandy stepped in. "Mom says you're my imagintary friend," said Mandy, "but you don't look like it."

Zoe closed the book. "What do imaginary friends look like?"

"They look nice," said Mandy. "Want some?" She held out her half-eaten banana.

"No, thanks," said Zoe. "So I don't look nice to you?"

"Nope," said Mandy through a mouthful of banana. "And you're not imagintary, anyways." Zoe tried to think fast as Mandy twirled her banana peel.

"You're right," said Zoe. "I'm not imaginary. I'm magical."

"What can you do?" said Mandy.

"Magical things," said Zoe.

"Like what?"

"I can make part of your house appear in my pocket,"

"Show me," said Mandy.

Zoe pulled out the triangle of wallpaper. Mandy pursed her lips as she peered at the poppies. "That's from my room," she said.

"Your room? Isn't that going to be your sister's?"

"Nope," said Mandy. "She's going to get the other one downstairs."

Zoe registered this new information. Mandy in her old room. Jessica in Juke's.

"What else can you do?" asked Mandy.

"What?"

"What more kinds of magic?"

"I can turn you into a frog if you tell people I'm up here."

"I like frogs," said Mandy with enthusiasm.

"You wouldn't like being one."

"Frogs are fun."

"You wouldn't be able to live inside your house anymore."

Mandy stopped wiggling her banana peel.

"And you wouldn't be able to see your mommy or daddy or play with your friends ever again."

"You're a mean magical girl," said Mandy with a nod.

"Just keep it a secret that I'm up here," said Zoe.

The kitchen door opened down below. Mrs. Jacobs poked her head out and shouted over the loud sawing sound. "Mandy! It's almost time for your bus!"

"You'd better leave," said Zoe.

Mandy held out her peel. "Turn this into a snake."

"I don't want to," said Zoe.

"Then you're not magical, you're just a girl stranger."

"I can read your mind."

"Okay," said Mandy.

"You're thinking about garden snakes."

"What colors are they?" said Mandy, crossing her arms.

"Green," said Zoe. "And the color dirty."

Mandy did a little dance with her feet. "Can I make a wish on you?"

"No wishes," said Zoe. "Unless you keep me a secret."

"Can you make me fly?" asked Mandy.

"Your mom wants you now," said Zoe. Mandy dropped her peel on the floor and waited. Zoe reached into her pocket and pulled out Georgia's pink feather. "It's a small feather, so it won't lift you up real high," whispered Zoe. "But you'll feel a floatingness in your feet."

Mandy bit her lip and nodded excitedly.

"And no jumping from high places," said Zoe. "That's just cheating."

Mandy left, pinching the pink feather in her small fingers. Zoe peered out the window and smiled to herself as she watched Mandy walk slowly down the garden steps, her arms outstretched like wings.

Down by the back corner of the house the whir of the table saw went suddenly silent. The carpenters leaned against the worktable. The one closest to Zoe looked tall enough to play pro basketball, but he'd have to ditch his potbelly first. He bummed a cigarette off the short guy with the curly hair, and they both lit up. Zoe watched the gray smoke trails rise and twirl above their heads like they were making miniature clouds. A night of zero sleep finally overtook her, and she curled up in a small patch of sunlight.

In her dream she flew over her house. It looked as small as a postage stamp from way up in the sky, but she cut through the air, whirled round and round like a hawk wheeling in the sky, then landed on the chimney. Big puffs of smoke belched from the brick mouth. Zoe coughed and woke up. She'd slept an hour, maybe more. The patch of sun she'd fallen asleep in had moved across the floor, but golden light flickered on the window. *Bad way to end a flying dream,* she thought, rubbing her eyes. But when she sat up, she saw the source of the smell that had invaded her dream right outside through the storage-room window.

Fire!

32

The woodpile was in flames! Piles of sawdust were sparking like fireworks and the back corner of the house was alight! She raced down the garage steps, turning back to check the driveway as she ran. No car, and the carpenters' truck hadn't returned. Probably their stupid cigarettes had started it. She ran down the garden path to the left side of the house, cranked on the hose, and sprayed the woodpile.

Waves of heat hit her face and body. The hose water was a slender spray of nothing. The wood hissed where it was hit, but the flames were too thick and greedy. Her spray of water was like a toy sword against a raging monster. She turned and sprayed the corner of the house. Who cared about the woodpile, anyway. This was her old bedroom! Her old window! The white walls were yellow and pulsing where the fire blazed. The wood was charred where it left a dead, black trail.

Zoe screamed and threw down the hose. She had to get to a phone and fast. It didn't matter that it wasn't her house anymore, just that it was burning. She couldn't let that happen even if it belonged to the Jacobses now. She raced up the back steps and tried the kitchen door. Locked. She flew down the walkway to the front door. Locked. Around the right side of the house to every reachable window. Locked. Locked. Locked. Back around to the front again. Where was everyone? Didn't anyone else see that the house was burning? She raced the tree-lined path to Kellen's house next door. Empty. No way in. Zoe flew home again.

Back at the kitchen window now, she peered through the glass. The telephone rested on the counter. She blinked again. Oh, man! Skittle was hiding under the kitchen table. She'd forgotten about the cat. The fire wasn't upstairs yet, but he had to get out fast. They used to have a hidden key by the kitchen door. Maybe the Jacobses did too? The crackling sound of burning wood from down below filled her ears. Why did it have to start near her room? She checked under the doormat and under the planter, then felt along the downspout for a magnet box. Nothing. A key stone, then? She reached under the steps and pulled out rock after rock, checking the back of each one for a little metal door before hurling it down the hill into the fire. In the seventh rock she found a tiny metal door. Hand shaking, she slid it open, grabbed the key, and shoved it in the keyhole.

The door opened. Smoke was creeping up from

downstairs, but the fire hadn't reached this floor yet. She shouldn't go in. She had to go in. Zoe darted into the kitchen, grabbed the mobile phone, raced back out the door, and dialed 911. "Fire!" she screamed. "18 Hawk Road! It's my house! The Jacobses' house! My house!"

The woman on the phone asked her questions, but Zoe couldn't think straight. "What? No one's inside! Just come!" she screamed. "Come now!" She pressed the OFF button and peered back inside.

"Skittle! Where are you?" A thin trail of smoke snaked across the kitchen floor. Skittle poked his head around the pantry door.

"Here, kitty," she called. "Come on." She knew better than to go back inside. But the cat backed farther against the wall. Two green eyes peered out at her.

"Come here, kitty," said Zoe. "I don't want to leave you here. Stupid cat!" She knelt down outside the door. "Skittle, please," she said in a softer tone. She reached out her hand, and Skittle slunk toward her. "Got ya!" Zoe swept him into her arms and ran up the garden steps.

Back up on Hawk Road she leaned against the picket fence and held Skittle tight as she listened to the sirens. "Faster! Faster!" she was saying as she heard the trucks winding up the narrow road. Then they came around the corner, red and roaring, bright lights flashing. Firefighters leaped off the trucks with thick gray hoses and raced past Zoe, shouting to one another as they ran down the garden steps.

Skittle clawed Zoe's arm, but she held him close,

watching the firehoses come alive like giant eels with water spouting from their mouths. *Save the house. Don't let it burn.* She thought the words over and over as she saw two firefighters rush to the kitchen door. Three more men ran down to the back corner of the house and sprayed the tall bright flames coming from her bedroom. *Don't let it burn!*

On the road behind Zoe the carpenters' truck pulled up. The curly-haired guy stepped out of the truck. "Wow, Ron, check it out!"

Ron climbed out and stood next to Zoe. "Jeez," he whispered. Zoe stepped aside to get away from the stink of Ron's sweaty shirt. He was close to seven feet, and his arms were as thick and solid as oak branches. The curly-haired guy lit a cigarette with a buck horn lighter and took a deep drag. Zoe stared at the small flame in disbelief. He was lighting up now? The carpenter took a deep drag. Zoe's throat constricted. Smoke billowed up from her house. Smoke from the cigarette. She felt a sudden flash of rage at the man and his stupid buckhorn lighter that had probably started the fire.

"Put it out, Keith," whispered Ron.

Keith ignored him and took another puff. Ron snatched the cigarette from Keith's hand, threw it down, and crushed it with his boot.

"Hey!" said Keith.

"Shut up!" said Ron.

The lady firefighter stepped up to the carpenters. She wasn't much taller than Zoe, so she had to crook her neck to look at Ron. "You fellows know anything about this fire?" she asked, pulling out a metal clipboard.

"No," said Ron.

Zoe's heart raced. Liar!

"Just here for the show, then?"

"We were working on the house," said Keith.

"I see," said the firefighter. "And when did you last see it?"

"Before there was a fire," said Keith.

"But you were here today?"

"We worked until noon, then took off for lunch," said Ron, stepping in front of Keith.

Ask them about the cigarettes, thought Zoe. She sent the telepathic message to the lady firefighter, but her yellow helmet must have intercepted it because it didn't reach her head.

"Any idea how this might have started?" she asked.

"No," said Ron. He leaned over the lady firefighter like a giant looking down at a troublesome dwarf. "Say," he said, "is this like a legal statement, because we didn't do anything wrong here."

"Yeah," said Keith. "And, anyway, what kind of retard would turn a good job into a cinder pile?"

"Quiet, Keith," said Ron, "I'll handle this."

Zoe touched the lady's slick yellow coat. The firefighter leaned in so close that Skittle started to purr.

"Yes?"

Zoe didn't want to look her in the face, so she

addressed the silver tape on her yellow helmet. "They were smoking by the woodpile."

"I see," said the firefighter.

Ron flexed his muscles like maybe he'd like to take a swing at her. But she'd read about giants in books, and they all had one thing in common: Each and every one of them was a moron.

"You know," said Zoe, "they were always taking these smoking breaks right down there." She pointed to what was left of the burned woodpile.

The firefighter wrote something on her clipboard. "Were you the caller?"

Zoe nodded.

"What's your name?"

"Zoe."

"Where did you call from, Zoe?"

"I went into the kitchen for the phone and —"

"You went inside a burning house?" Her chin jutted out. "You know you should never endanger yourself that way!"

"I'm . . . I'm sorry."

"Just remember, honey, people are more important than houses."

Zoe looked down and prodded Keith's cigarette butt with her sneaker. Totally unfair. Here she was getting lectured while Ron and Keith stood by and watched. Smoke rose up the hill. She coughed and leaned against the fence.

The firefighter turned to the carpenters. "Names, please?" she said.

"I'm Ron and this is Keith."

"Okay, stick around here, guys, while we try to sort this out."

Zoe steered clear of Ron. She could feel his eyes peeling off the back of her skull, but he couldn't do anything to her as long as she stayed close to the fire trucks. Her throat was sore and her eyes were stinging, but she couldn't look away. The first story on the back side of the house was still on fire. Arcs of water dousing it sent smoke billowing up. Her whole past down there. Burning.

Zoe hadn't seen the Jacobses' van pull up, so she didn't know they were home until she heard Mrs. Jacobs. "Oh my God!" she cried as she pulled her daughters close to her. Zoe felt Mandy brush against her as they huddled together, all of them crying now as the fire roared below. Firefighters shouted. Hoses hissed. Flames leaped from the rear of the house to the redwoods. Zoe's whole body began to shake. Her bones were going all to straw like the Scarecrow in Oz. Any second now her knees were going to go out from under her. She hugged Skittle to her chest and let the tears fall. Zoe watched the trees below as one by one the deep green branches put on sudden yellow scarves.

"Your house?" asked the lady firefighter.

Mrs. Jacobs sniffed and nodded. The lady checked a

page on her clipboard. "Your daughter called and said her house was burning."

"My . . . my daughter?"

"Give me Skittle Cat," said Mandy.

"Hey," said Mrs. Jacobs. "I remember you." She peered at Zoe with puffy eyes. "We met the day we toured the house. You're the girl who used to live here."

Now everyone was looking at Zoe—the firefighter, tipping her head; Mrs. Jacobs and her girls with questioning eyes.

"You said she was my imagintary friend," said Mandy, "but she's magical."

"Well, she's certainly magical," said the firefighter. "Her early call has probably saved your house."

Zoe wiped her wet cheek and looked from face to face. Her cover was blown, but it didn't matter now. It was time to come out of hiding.

33

In Kellen's kitchen Zoe dialed Dad's cell phone number while Kellen and her parents watched. Dad's phone rang twice.

"Hello?"

"It's me," said Zoe.

"How'd the science project go?" asked Dad. When she didn't answer, he said, "Ready to be picked up from Aliya's?"

"I'm not at Aliya's."

"Okay," said Dad. "Where do I meet you, then?"

"Tillerman."

Dad laughed. Zoe didn't. The phone buzzed as he took in the news. "What in God's name are you doing in Tillerman?"

Zoe handed the phone to Kellen's dad. "Yeah, Hap, that's right," said Mr. Farley. "Oh, she says she took the bus down. And she's been here a couple of days." Mr.

Farley stared at his warped reflection in the toaster. "What? No. I only just found out myself. She's been kind of hiding out from us all." He paused. "Yes, I know it's pretty upsetting, Hap, but I think we've just got a bad case of homesickness here."

Kellen's mom patted Zoe's shoulder, and Kellen squeezed her hand. Zoe wanted to jump out of her skin.

"Yeah, she can stay at our house till you get here," said Mr. Farley. "Oh, sure, it's no problem." Mr. Farley cleared his throat. "Uh, there is one more thing, Hap. It's about your old house." He stepped to the window and looked out. "18 Hawk Road caught fire." Zoe felt her blood rushing down to her feet.

"No. No one was hurt. As a matter of fact, Zoe called it in. There's some damage to the downstairs, but the rest of the house is fine. They've just got some rebuilding to do." He smiled. "Yeah, I know. She's a brave kid. The Jacobses might have lost everything if it hadn't been for her."

Mrs. Farley reached for the receiver.

"My wife wants to say a word." He turned to look at Zoe. "Sure thing. She'll be fine with us. Okay, I'll see you soon."

Mr. Farley handed the phone to Mrs. Farley. She leaned against the kitchen counter. "Hello, Hap?"

"I gotta use the bathroom," said Zoe. She broke free from Kellen and headed down the hall. The water ran clear across her sooty hands. She waited for the ringing in her ears to stop, steam rising up all around her until the girl in the mirror disappeared.

Right after the phone call Kellen's mom took over. She ran Zoe a bath, gave her fresh clothes, and treated her to a special spaghetti dinner. Later she sent the girls off to Kellen's room with a plateful of cookies. A definite first.

Kellen's room was just the same. Books, laundry, stuffed animals, a zillion shoes spread all over the floor. Kellen sat cross-legged on her bed with the plate of oatmeal cookies in her lap. "You're a hero," she said between bites. "You might even end up in the papers."

"You think so?" Zoe didn't feel like a hero. She'd blown it a hundred times over in the past few months. "I was just trying to . . . to . . ." She frowned and looked out the night-dark window.

"It was pretty cool of you to save the Jacobses' house."

Zoe pushed the cookie crumbs around on the plate.

"But you shouldn't have gone inside to get their phone. You should have made the call from here." Kellen bit her cookie thoughtfully.

"The doors were locked over here."

"Oh, yeah. Well, if you'd had a cell phone, you could've used that. They're good for emergencies, my mom always says."

Zoe shifted position on the bed. It was weird. Here they were sitting together just like they had a thousand times before, and it was all awkward between them. She chose a cookie and plucked a raisin from the middle. Maybe she shouldn't blame Kellen for the distance.

She'd written a couple of letters while she was gone, but she'd never told her the truth about Scout River; never said that she'd been living in the van for all those months while she was away. Friendships got kind of strained when you tried to keep big secrets like that.

Kellen glanced at Zoe, then looked away. "So you've been hiding out in your dad's old study since Saturday morning?" she said. "And you didn't even come by to see me?"

Zoe didn't want to bring up seeing her with Jessica. It felt like old news now. And, anyway, she'd made a new friend herself since she'd been gone.

Kellen twisted the comforter and waited for an answer.

"I was hiding out from everyone," said Zoe.

"Even from me?"

"Yeah, you know. Like spies do." Zoe got up on her knees and took Black Beauty down from the shelf above the bed. He was kind of dusty but otherwise okay.

"I never let Meg touch him," said Kellen.

"Thanks." Zoe blew the dust off his mane.

Kellen sucked on a strand of hair. "You want him back?"

"What?" She looked into Kellen's green eyes. "No, I gave him to you. He's yours now." She slid Black Beauty back on Kellen's shelf. She'd had to let go of bigger things than a porcelain horse in the past few days.

The soft bed invited Zoe to lean back. She stared at the Background Noise posters on the wall; one photo of the guys with their guitars taken at Stonehenge, another in an alley leaning on their motorcycles.

Kellen leaped up. "Have you heard their latest CD? You've got to love it!" She put on the CD and pulled her nail-polish kit from the drawer. She was humming the song as she opened the plastic box lid. "Great, isn't it?" she said.

"Yeah," said Zoe. Kellen's face dropped. Zoe could tell Kellen was really trying to make things work, and her own flat responses weren't helping. But rock groups weren't quite so godlike for Zoe. She'd had her fill of Jam for Breakfast years ago. Kellen traced her hand along the color choices in her kit as the song changed.

"Oh, I like this one," said Zoe, and Kellen perked up.

"Yeah, it's one of their best songs. Orange toenails tonight or blue?" she asked, pointing to the bottles.

"Pink," said Zoe.

"Just like the pink moon?" teased Kellen.

"Shut up," said Zoe. But she felt herself smiling as Kellen unscrewed the nail-polish lid.

Zoe lay on the trundle bed just below Kellen. They'd talked for hours about all the dumb things they'd tried when they were little. "Remember the time you drank ketchup?" and "Remember the time your bike was stolen and the cops found it in a ditch?" and "Remember the race car we tried to make out of Juke's old stroller?"

Now Kellen was asleep. Zoe stared at the glow-in-the-dark stars on the ceiling. It was strange. The whole time they were laughing about the kid stuff they'd done, and even while Kellen listed off all the cute boys at school, Zoe's mind had kept wandering off in the direction of Scout River. She kept thinking about Aliya.

34

Mom and Dad arrived in the middle of the night and crept past Kellen's room. Shadows passed. Dad carrying Juke, Mom loaded down with the sleeping bags. A moment later Mom and Dad tiptoed up to Zoe's bed and kissed her on the cheek. She breathed long and deep, pretending she was somewhere down inside a dream. Dad touched her eyebrow. "Good night, princess," he said.

After an early breakfast they had "the talk" in Kellen's room. Just Mom and Dad and Zoe while Juke played upstairs with Meg and Kellen.

"So," said Dad, "tell us everything."

Zoe told them about the bus ride, her hideout above the garage. She left out her plans to release a rat in the Jacobses' house. Who had to know that? She was just talking about the fire when Mom started crying. Zoe hugged her, and Dad put his arms around them both.

"We love you so much, honey," said Mom. "And we *will* get a place for you. It just can't be our old house here on Hawk Road."

"I know," said Zoe.

"Don't run off like that again," whispered Dad.

"I won't."

Mom and Dad went out to talk to Kellen's parents while Zoe repacked her bag. You could retrieve a lost ball that went over a fence. You could reclaim your stolen bike down at the police station if the cops were good enough to find it for you. But you couldn't retrieve a house. You couldn't take back something so big, even if it belonged to you once. But then, maybe it wasn't her house she'd been trying to rescue. Maybe it was her old life.

The Flynns said a quick good-bye to the Farleys. Two hugs for Kellen at the door and one more at the van. At the edge of town Dad pulled over to fill the empty tank. Pump in hand, he stood in the soft morning wind, the yellow gas station light catching the gold in his earring, and just like that, Zoe was back. It wasn't so much the look on Dad's face but the moment itself that threw her because it was a total déjà vu.

Five months ago she'd waited in the cramped van while he filled the tank for their trip. The lines in his face had caught the light, just like this. Juke had chewed a wad of gum, just like this. Mom had waited, silent, just like this. And she'd leaned her head against the window, trying to get a last look at Fletcher Park, just the way she was doing now. Somehow the same moment had repeated in time and space. A rerun of letting go as the numbers on the gas pump rolled higher and higher. Dad holding the hose, filling it to the brim. Fuel for leaving Tillerman behind.

A moment later they merged back into the morning traffic. Pretty soon they'd hit the coast road and head up north. Only this time Zoe knew where they were going.

35

All the unfinished business Zoe had left behind in Scout River was waiting for her when she got back. And that included a certain letter from Einstein Elementary lurking in the P.O. box. Unfortunately, Dad beat Zoe to it, and he opened Ms. Eagle's progress report before she could weasel it away from him. Dad eyeballed the page, passed it to Mom, and said exactly five words: "Things are going to change."

The very next afternoon Zoe had sat in the little alcove at the public library and stared at the stack of unfinished schoolwork. She felt like the girl in the fairy tale who was told she must spin a room full of straw into gold overnight, only she didn't have a magical little dude named Rumpelstiltskin to help her out. Mom and Dad had been firm. After school each day when she finished her poodle-walking job, she was expected to hightail it straight to the library and put in two hours of schoolwork until she was caught up.

Today was her third day working on the paper pile, and she wasn't making much headway. Armed with sharp pencils and a thick eraser, she was bound to finish history, geography, science, and math papers, shrinking the stack page by page until every single missing assignment was turned in.

She figured it would take roughly two thousand years, but Ms. Eagle had set the deadline at two weeks. Zoe sighed and slid the science paper titled "What Are Atoms?" from the stack. *Atoms are tiny bits of matter,* she read. Well, she knew that. *One million atoms could fit in the period at the end of this sentence.* Okay, she didn't know that.

Twenty minutes later the science page was done, and the million billion atoms at the tips of her fingers were itching to try something else. She pulled out the math packet. In some ways having all this makeup work was a good thing. It kept her busy every day after school so she didn't have to think about Aliya.

Mallory had blown it for her big time when she pointed out that Aliya had never been to her house. It had always been a sore point. Now a wall had gone up between them. The only way past the wall would be to break the family secret and tell Aliya the real reason she'd never been invited over, and Zoe couldn't do that. Meanwhile, Aliya had made friends with Trish, a girl who wore pink braces and was animal crazy. They'd gone to each other's houses, and Trish had already made beaded collars for Aliya's cats.

Zoe focused on her fraction paper. She would bury her thoughts of Aliya under mountains of math problems. Problem one: *If a 13" x 9" brownie pan is divided into 20 equal-size brownies, what are the dimensions of one brownie?* Her stomach rumbled as she sucked on her pencil, twenty equal-size brownies dancing before her eyes.

36

It was early yet, and the sun was just
rising above the mountains. A soft pink light fell across
the van window, thin as a fairy's scarf. Zoe pulled on her
jeans and coat and slipped out the passenger door. The
wet smell of late-November rain was still in the air, but
the morning was clear. She took the trail out to the edge
of the woods and climbed her favorite boulder.

Sunlight swept up the hill on the far side of town,
turning the windows of the houses into gold. Zoe
remembered the first time she'd seen golden windows.
She was four, maybe five, and they'd gotten up early to
go to the morning service. On the way to church she'd
seen the houses on the hill, all their windows shining,
and she'd screamed out, "Daddy! Take me there!"

Dad told her the windows weren't gold. It was only
the sunlight she was seeing, but she hadn't believed him.
She'd wanted him to take her to the magic city, and he'd

refused. It wasn't until they were driving home that same morning that she saw he was right. The windows facing east across the hill were as empty and dark as crow's eyes.

Zoe squinted at the golden homes, trying to find Aliya's. It was hard to tell at such a distance, but she found it at last, the thee gables on the roof giving it away. A hawk flew over the river and up the hill to the graveyard, its wings sending small dark shadows across the gravestones. It was then that Zoe saw the policeman. He was standing a few hundred feet below, his head bent before a gravestone. He held a small bouquet in his hands, his blue uniform looking almost black in the early light. When he lifted his head, Zoe dropped down flat on the damp boulder. Officer Bergstrom. She'd know that blond head and those mirrored sunglasses anywhere. Had he seen her standing above on the boulder?

Zoe slowly lifted her head and wiped the dirt from her cheek. Officer Bergstrom was down on one knee now, putting flowers on the grave. He looked at the line of trees to the right of the graveyard, then stood up and scanned the hill where Zoe hid.

A small dot of light crossed the boulder, the reflection of his mirrored glasses. She held the rock and waited. A moment later Officer Bergstrom turned and walked back through the tailored grass to the lower parking lot and got into his patrol car. It wasn't until he drove through the iron gate and turned down Cascade Drive that Zoe felt safe to stand again. She carefully climbed down the high hillside until she came to the cemetery's iron fence. Walking along the edge of the fence, she slipped through the gate, then headed across the lawn looking for footprints. Some clue that would lead her to the right gravestone. But the damp grass gave no sign. Zoe looked back up at the boulders on the hill, trying to make out the direction from there, then she tried the row of gravestones on her right. Halfway down the row she spotted the small bouquet he'd left behind and came to the place where he'd been standing.

Her mouth went dry and her skin felt tight, as if it were suddenly a size too small for the girl inside. Officer Bergstrom hadn't brought roses and baby's breath to an old person's grave, someone who'd died of a heart attack at age ninety-five. This was the grave of an eleven-year-old kid.

"Julia Bergstrom," she whispered. The name brought the man behind the sunglasses and the smiling girl she'd seen in the photos together in her mind.

Father and daughter seemed like opposites, but she'd seen something in his blue eyes the time when he'd removed his shades to warn her. "Promise me you'll obey all the bike laws," he'd said. "Wear your bike helmet. And get off your bike on that steep hill leading down to the bridge."

She'd promised him, feeling afraid of his strength and confused by the kindness in his eyes. He was asking her to do what his daughter hadn't done. Wear her helmet. Fear the speed of the cars. Avoid the thrill of the steep hill, when the bike flies so fast that the wind smacks your face and fills your baggy T-shirt like a sail.

Zoe stood so still, she could hear the wind coming toward her. She hadn't known Julia the way Aliya had. But she'd seen the girl in the photos. Julia on the deck. Julia on horseback flashing a crooked smile. And she'd imagined her at Shepherd's Glen, sitting up on the fence as she sketched Ali Baba on the run.

Zoe looked around the close-cropped grass for a stray wildflower to lay on the grave. Nothing there, but there was something in her pocket. She pulled out the piece of flowered wallpaper she'd taken from her old bedroom and placed it beside Officer Bergstrom's bouquet. A small triangular strip of California poppies.

37

Aliya was sitting alone in the lunchroom.
Zoe placed her lunch sack on the table. "Guess what?"
Aliya didn't look up, but Zoe kept going. "I saw Officer
Bergstrom in the graveyard the other day. He was put-
ting roses on Julia's grave."

Aliya pulled at the corner of her milk carton.

"Why didn't you tell me he was her dad?"

"I didn't know you knew him."

"I've seen him lots of times," said Zoe. "He's always
following me around when I'm on my bike."

It was the wrong thing to say. He'd probably been
checking out a lot of kids on their bikes since the acci-
dent. Aliya looked down and went back to her battle with
the milk carton.

"Here," said Zoe. "Sometimes they stick. You can use
your fork to pry it open." She poked Aliya's plastic fork
into the corner of the carton and broke a tine, but the

corner finally gave way. Zoe laid the broken fork on the orange tray. The door opened, and the third and fourth graders stampeded into the lunchroom.

"Here come the elephants," said Zoe. She and Aliya had called them that from week one. Aliya didn't look up or give away a smile.

Things weren't going the way Zoe had planned. She'd wanted to sit next to her and talk in quiet whispers about finding Julia's grave.

"What were you doing up at the graveyard?" said Aliya.

Zoe reached for something that wouldn't give away the family secret. "I was . . ." *Quick, think of something!* "I was walking my dog."

"Your dog?"

"Dogs are great," said Trish, coming up from behind to put her tray down next to Aliya's. "What's your dog's name?"

"Merlin," said Zoe.

"Aliya has three cats. All white. There's Bijlee, Billo, and Rustham. They love the beaded collars I made them." Trish spread her smile across her pink braces.

"I know her cats," said Zoe. She wanted to say she knew Bijlee, Billo, and Rustham much better than Trish ever would. They'd curled up on her lap hundreds of times, and she knew how to get them purring.

Aliya tugged her straw out of its paper sleeve. "Merlin," she said, crumpling the paper. "You've come to my house lots of times and played with my cats and given them treats." She looked up at Zoe for the first time since she'd come over to the table. "You never said you had a dog." Zoe felt the sting of Aliya's dark eyes.

"What kind of dog is he?" asked Trish.

"A golden retriever."

"Oh," said Trish, licking cheese sauce off her plastic spoon. "Great dogs. They're totally loyal."

The noisy lunchroom seemed suddenly quiet, the word *loyal* thrumming in the air between Zoe and Aliya, as still and beating as a hummingbird's wings. Then Trish cinched it by saying the one thing Zoe had never been able to say. "So, can you come to my house today?"

Aliya turned to her and smiled. "Sure. I'd like that."

Zoe grabbed her lunch and backed away from the table. End of conversation. End of reason to stick around in the lunchroom. She went outside to hang around with the maple trees.

38

Juke drank the milk from his metal camping bowl. "Almost Christmas," he said between slurps. Mom collected the empty bowls.

"I want a tree like we get every year," said Juke.

"We have lots of trees," said Mom. "They're all around us."

"I mean the kind you decorate."

Zoe peered out the van window. Most of the evergreens were way too tall for Christmas trees, but they picked up the morning wind and waved their branches in a friendly way like the redwoods behind her old bedroom.

Dad rolled up the sleeping bags and prepared to head out of camp. "Ready?" he said. "Seat belts, everyone."

"In our old house," Juke was saying as they rumbled down the dirt road, "we always got to have a big tree with lots of decorations and candy canes and stuff." The van chugged onto Cascade Drive and motored past the iron graveyard fence. "And popcorn strands with cranberries sometimes."

"Shut up, Juke," said Zoe.

"Zoe," said Mom. "Be nice."

Zoe leaned over and whispered, "Just shut up about Christmas, Juke. Understand?" The van splashed through a puddle. Brown water sprayed out from the tires. Zoe hoped they'd go to the Laundromat first. It was always warm there. You could hang out near the dryers and feel the heat cover your whole body like a blast of sweet tropical wind. Bring a mango shake with her, and she could almost be at Aliya's house again. Anyway, she'd have the taste of it.

Down the hill Dad turned left and followed the curve of Scout River.

"I thought we were going to town?" said Juke.

"Got a stop to make first," said Dad.

They sped along till they came to the chain-link fence of the mobile home park and drove through the gate. Zoe caught a glimpse of a dishwasher sitting in the mud before slumping down in her seat. Great. Dad's new best friend, Mel, had to live here, of course. And Dad had to swap the latest science fiction books with him, of course. Well, he better not take too long. Shelia might be playing outside.

"Gabe's house!" yelled Juke. "Can I go see him?"

"All right," said Dad, "but don't be long."

Juke leaped outside and raced down the dirt road to Gabe's. Zoe slammed the van door shut from the inside and lay low. It would be over soon. She'd just have to wait it out. Unless Dad got to talking about his favorite science fiction author, Ray Bradbury, with Mel. Dad could talk about Ray Bradbury for a zillion years without taking a breath.

Suddenly Mom reached around the front seat and tugged a brush across Zoe's head.

"Ouch, Mom. Stop it."

"Your hair's a mess," said Mom.

"So what?" Zoe slumped farther down, but Mom caught her arm.

"Sit up," said Mom. "Enough with the passive resistance. This isn't a political demonstration."

Two things appeared in the window when Zoe sat up. The first was the sight of Juke down the lane climbing into an old rowboat sandbox. The second was Dad talking to a man in front of a blue mobile home. The sign in the darkened window read FOR RENT.

39

It turned out Dad hadn't come to the mobile home park to meet Mel. He'd come to meet the manager. Big surprise! The manager turned the key and let them all inside. The living room smelled like mushrooms. Maybe it was the old brown carpet, or maybe it was the three-legged stuffed chair the previous renters had left abandoned by the front window. Zoe skirted the chair and stayed behind Mom and Dad as the manager showed them around. Mom inspected the cupboards in the little kitchen off the front room. Then they traipsed down the hall to peer at the bathroom and check out the bedrooms.

Mom was just nodding at a brown spot on the bedroom carpet as if she were deciding what brand of carpet foam she'd use to clean up the stain when Juke ran down the hall. "Mom, Dad, hey!" he called, coming through the doorway. "I really gotta go!"

Mom led Juke to the bathroom and closed the door behind him. Zoe leaned against the cold bedroom wall. What was that smell? It was way worse than mushrooms. More like rotten cabbages.

"The most reasonable rent in town," the manager was saying as he abandoned the smaller room to show off the master bedroom. "Beats an apartment any day, and folks can hear the river at night. Makes for good comfort."

Dad opened the blinds that looked out on the mobile home next door, then closed them again. Seven stripes of sunlight on the floor shrunk to razor-thin lines, then disappeared. A stampede of warnings rushed through Zoe's mind. *We can't live here! Not in the trailer park! Anywhere else in town is better! Anywhere!*

Juke slammed the bathroom door and raced up the hall, colliding into her and jamming her against the doorframe on his way to Dad's arms. "Are we moving here? Right next to Gabe? All right!"

"Looks like you've got a happy camper," said the manager. Then, seeing Zoe tug her coat tighter around her middle, he stooped to turn on the electric wallboard heater. "We'll be warmed up in a jiffy," he said.

Mom put her arm around Zoe and smiled at the empty room. "What do you think, honey?"

"Just a minute," said Zoe. She beat it down the narrow hall to the bathroom, where she locked the door, used the toilet, then held her hands under the warm running water at the sink. The dark-haired girl in the mirror with the big brown eyes used to live in an old two-story house. The house was white on the outside and creamy white on the inside.

Upstairs on Sunday mornings the light slid through the big living-room windows like bright water, the old glass making white wave patterns on the hardwood floors. There was silence there when everyone else was sleeping. Silence so thick, you could swim in it. The brown-haired, brown-eyed girl belonged in that light as much as a selkie belonged in the sea. She didn't belong in a cluttered van or a smelly mobile home. Zoe shut off the faucet and let her hands drip into the sink.

"I gotta tell Gabe!" Juke called as he raced past the bathroom door.

"Wait up, Juke," said Dad. "We haven't heard from Zoe yet."

Zoe dried her hands on her pants. She'd have to tell them *No way* before Dad shook hands with the manager. She'd have to make it clear that she could never be one of the trailer kids. "Okay," she whispered, nodding to the mirror. She joined the family in the living-room.

"Isn't it great?" said Juke. Dad was smiling ear to ear. Mom was smiling too. Juke hopped up and down, then sprang forward throwing his arms out wide. "It's big, isn't it?" he yelled, spinning around faster and faster till he toppled to the floor.

"Bigger than the van," said Zoe.

The manager laughed. "Of course it's bigger than your van! It's a mobile home." The word *home* seemed to shake Mom up. Her eyes suddenly brimmed with tears. She blinked them away, then smiled at Zoe.

"I was thinking about Christmas," said Dad.

"Only two weeks away," said the manager.

"A Christmas tree!" said Juke. "A big one right here!" He jumped up and pointed to a spot in the corner by the broken chair.

"Where would you put the tree, Zoe?" said Dad.

Zoe was going to say *Anywhere but in this stupid mobile home,* but with everyone's eyes on her, full of hope and wishes, and with Juke now drawing a big imaginary circle in the air where he thought the Christmas tree should stand, she fought against her impulse to run out the front door and walked over to her brother. "I think . . ." Zoe looked at her mom, her dad. Dad took a deep breath as if he were about to blow something her way. "I think Juke's picked a good spot," she said.

Mom rushed across the room and hugged her so hard, she could barely swallow against her mom's bony shoulder. She put her mouth to Zoe's ear. "Thank you," she whispered.

A couple of days later they moved into their new mobile home. Well, not exactly new, just empty. Right away Mom went into cleaning mode, and the place smelled pretty good when they were done. Kind of a pinewood scent with a little window cleaner after-smell. Zoe quickly learned that the people who lived in her new neighborhood didn't call it a trailer park. They called it

River View, the name painted on the wooden sign wired to the sagging chain-link fence. She chose the bedroom at the far end of the hall because she could see the storage shed out her back window. The small wooden shed had a corrugated tin roof, two little windows, and a bright red door.

The manager had shown it to them, saying, "And here's a place for all your extra things." Mom had looked at Dad and smiled. Extra things? They had zippo. But the manager didn't know that. He'd talked on and on about how everyone at River View loved their storage sheds. "And they're all stuffed to the gills," he said proudly. "Most mobile home parks don't have them, but here at River View we provide the sheds. No extra charge."

He unlocked the shed and swung the door wide. Zoe crossed the small dusty room that smelled of cedarwood and peered out the little window at the back. Through the fence and a thick stand of trees, she saw a handful of diamonds on the river. Dad called her back outside, and she pulled away from the window, but not before she felt a tingling in her fingertips.

40

On Thursday night Max pulled up outside in a U-Haul. Zoe stood at the back of the truck as the ramp lowered like a drawbridge. Boxes and furniture were crammed in the dim interior. Far in the back something moved. A black nose emerged from the dog carrier behind the couch. Then Merlin wiggled his way past a box and trotted down the ramp.

Suddenly Zoe and Juke were all over him, tumbling in the tall grass, wrapping him in arms and legs, and body wrestling with him till he was barking, wild and happy and confused. Heart pounding, Zoe leaned against Merlin, breathing in the bitter-clean smells of grass and dirt. She kissed his soft ear. "I told you," she said. "I told you I wouldn't forget." He panted happily, his tail measuring a big wide arc of doggie bliss.

"Look at all this!" said Mom, climbing up the ramp. Dad and Max followed her up and came out with Dad's dresser and desk! Next came Juke's dresser! Zoe's dresser from her old room! The little Swedish coffee table! The rocking chair Grandma Nell had given them! Then Dad and Max came down the ramp hefting the rolled-up carpet!

"Wait," called Mom. "We need to roll it out before we start arranging the furniture." Zoe and Juke came inside with Merlin, who seemed as interested in rolling out the carpet as Dad and Max.

"Keep him back, will you, Zoe?" said Dad.

Zoe held Merlin's collar, his tail thwacking her leg as the carpet rolled across the floor.

"It fits!" said Mom, smiling.

"Practically fills up the whole room," said Max.

Dad gave Mom a hug before they headed back out for more stuff. Juke and Merlin ran after, but Zoe stole a minute alone in the almost-empty room. She'd been right about Aliya's carpet; it had a similar design, but Grandma's was more faded. Probably older. She lay belly down on the rug. Here were her golden snow-peaked mountains. And here the diamond shapes touched, forming into horses that galloped across the red plains. She sniffed the wool and found a sort of storage-room smell from Max's house. She scrambled to another corner and sniffed again. At the third corner she hit pay dirt. There it was, the sweet-dry smell of chamomile. The rug remembered.

That night Merlin came into her room and put his paws on the windowsill. Zoe closed the door and stood beside him looking out at the twilight sky. The moon was out early. Just the smallest piece of it hanging over Scout River. "See it?" she said. Merlin looked up, catching a piece of moon in his brown eyes.

Her empty room was better now—her dresser here, her bookshelves, and Merlin. She wrapped her star quilt around her shoulders. It had been the very last thing to come out of the blanket box. She let the quilt's warmth flood through her. The moment slowed to silence. And magic, no bigger than the slender moon, came with it. With her star quilt tight around her, she felt like the selkie who'd left the sea and lost her skin. Now she had it back again.

41

This time, Zoe was the one doing the following. She'd seen Officer Bergstrom's patrol car turn right on Miller Avenue, so she walked Tiddlywink, Jinx, and Merlin around the corner. Three blocks down she spotted his car parked outside Galaxy Burgers.

"You guys be good," she warned as she tied the leashes to a spindly poplar tree on the sidewalk. The dogs lay down in the cold, golden winter sunshine. "That's right," said Zoe. She blew on her chilled fingers and pushed through the swinging glass door. Officer Bergstrom had already slid into one of the corner booths with a giant cookie and steaming cup of coffee. She gave him a quick glance and played with the straw dispenser. She should go over. Say something to him. But what?

The line moved forward, and as she scanned the meal selections her eye fell on five new words tacked to the bottom of the menu board. INTRODUCING THE VENUS

VEGGIE BURGER. Zoe blinked. Smiled. Blinked again. She hadn't won the Galaxy Game's Intergalactic Cash Prize back in November, but she couldn't help getting kind of warm all over as she read the new addition. They'd actually read her little blue sheet, and her note had made a difference! Nothing like that had ever happened to her back in Tillerman.

Frizzy Guy was tapping the counter. "You ready to order or what?"

"What? Oh, yeah. I'll take the Venus Veggie Burger."

"You want fries with that?"

"Sure!"

"One Venus with Orbit Fries!" shouted Frizzy Guy.

Zoe scooted into a booth across the aisle from Officer Bergstrom, but he never looked her way. She ate her burger, a breath of steam rising from the meatless middle. It sure was nice to have something more than a gob of relish and a paper-thin square of processed cheese inside the bun! Later she pocketed her fries and headed back outside.

Officer Bergstrom stood beside the spindly tree patting Jinx on the head. He turned around, paper coffee cup in hand, and looked down at Zoe. No sunglasses this time. "Nice dogs you've got here." He nodded at Merlin. "This one yours too?"

"Yeah," said Zoe. Merlin barked in agreement.

"Shush, Merlin," warned Zoe.

Officer Bergstrom bent down on one knee and gave Merlin a pat. "I think Merlin just wanted a pat on the head too." Zoe watched him rubbing Merlin's golden head. She wanted to say she was sorry about Julia, that she understood why he'd followed her when she was on her bike, that she had a house now, but it all became word salad in her head. She couldn't talk about Julia, and he hadn't really been following her, just worried about her safety, and she was sure now he'd never suspected that her family was living in their van. So all that came out was: "Merlin can catch a Frisbee in midair."

"I bet he can." Officer Bergstrom stood up kind of stiffly, the way Zoe imagined the Tin Man moving when he needed Dorothy to oil his joints.

He saw Zoe's questioning look, and he rubbed the small of his back. "I'm a little sore," he said. "I've been taking riding lessons."

"You?" said Zoe. Then she blushed. "I mean—"

"I know, it's kind of hard to imagine someone my age getting on a horse for the first time. My daughter . . ." He looked away and crushed his coffee cup. "She always wanted me to learn."

Now, thought Zoe. *Say something now.*

"Well, break's over," said Officer Bergstrom. "I've gotta be getting back." He stepped toward the patrol car.

"Hey," said Zoe. "I mean, well, good luck with the lessons."

"Yeah," he said. "I'll need it." He ran his hand through his blond crew cut and flashed her a crooked smile.

🚌

On Sunday after breakfast Dad brought his toolbox out to the storage shed. He opened the door and knelt down inside the shed. "Okay," he said, "now hand me the screwdriver." Zoe held the glass knob in place while Dad fed the screw into the tiny hole. "Hold it steady," he said.

She knelt down beside him on the wood floor and pressed a little harder. "Hope this works," she said.

"No problem," said Dad. "I know you've been waiting a long time for this."

"You don't mind that I took it, then?"

Dad let the question hang in the air for a moment while he slipped the second screw into the hole and began to twist it in place. "Well," he said, "the knob was your birthday present from Grandma Nell, wasn't it? I figure it was yours to keep." Zoe wanted to hug him, but she had to keep her hand steady on the knob.

Dad gave the second screw a final twist, then came to a stand. "Let's try it out," he said, stepping on the grass outside the shed. Zoe closed the door. Dad waited a moment, then knocked three times. She turned the glass knob and opened the door to his smile.

Dad headed back to the house with the toolbox, and Merlin trotted into the shed. "Like it?" asked Zoe. Merlin did a circle dance in the middle of the floor. "Yeah, it's a big place," agreed Zoe, turning to tug her old bookshelf closer to the wall. She'd hauled her books and drawing pad in from her bedroom, carried in her yellow beanbag chair, and last of all, she'd brought in Mandy's letter. Now with the door closed, she wedged herself in the corner. Merlin curled up at her feet, and she opened the letter for another read.

Dear Zoe,
Kellen told us your P.O. box address. My mom is writing this letter for me, and I'm telling her what to say because I don't write too many words yet. Thank you for saving our house from the fire. We have new carpenters now. Dad says my new room will be done by New Year's maybe. I lost my pink feather, so send me another.

Skittle says meow.

Your friend,
Mandy Jacobs

Mandy had signed the bottom of the letter and her printing filled up a two-inch space, but all the letters were about the same size, which was pretty good for a kindergarten kid. Zoe would have to visit Georgia at Pet Pals and ask where she bought those little pink feathers of hers. She slid the letter between a couple of books, the crayon signature still showing in the corner. If someone had to end up in her old bedroom, she was glad it would be Mandy.

Merlin was already asleep, his eyelids twitching in a

dream. She wiggled her toes under his warm weight, then slid open her box of colored chalks. Her fingers weren't tingling, but that didn't matter. Her hand knew what to do even if her brain didn't, and she let her hand have its way, filling page after page with drawings, some of her home in Tillerman, some of the places she'd been in Scout River. She drew people, too—Mandy playing in the dirt, Kellen on her back deck, Dad when he still had his ponytail. Then she colored Julia, yellow pastel for her short blond hair, blue for her tank top, etching the lines of the photograph from memory.

Her arm was tired, but she kept her chalk moving. It was as if all the things she'd been longing to draw since they'd left Tillerman last summer had been stored up in her body. Now the pictures were flooding from her chest, down her arm, and through her fingers. She bit her lip and watched the flow of colors streaming out of her pastels. Time slowed to the rhythm of her hand.

Now the brown chalk was drawing straight lines. Another house, 18 Hawk Road again, she thought, but then the roofline tilted suddenly and a whole new story went up. She added three gables to the roof, then filled in the windows with the same golden color she'd seen when she'd watched the house early one morning from across the river valley. Last she colored Aliya's window gold.

42

The final bell rang on the last day before winter break. It was Zoe's last chance to talk to Aliya. She turned in her seat and looked at the back row. Aliya saw her and pretended not to. She was packing her books, laughing and talking with Trish. Their conversation floated across the noisy classroom and tangled up in a spaghetti of sound. There was no way to tell what they were talking about, but it didn't matter. Zoe knew that the laughter and the "I'm so cool" looks were meant for her. It was like a bad after-school movie, and she was the target audience.

She watched a little longer: Trish looking in her direction and cracking a joke; Aliya nodding and smiling so wide, you could practically count all of her teeth. Then Zoe jammed the tiny Christmas ornament she'd been saving deeper in her pocket. She grabbed her backpack and headed out the door.

It was drizzling outside. The wind smelled of wet evergreens and slick sidewalks. She cornered the building and stepped over a multicolored puddle, the spill of gasoline mixing pink and blue and green. Cold metal stung her fingers as she spun her combination bike lock. She ignored the kids passing her on the sidewalk. Most of them had rides home on this wet day.

In the parking lot behind her a series of car doors slammed shut and motors purred to a start. She wrapped the chain lock around her bike frame and considered throwing the little Christmas ornament into the thornbush before pushing off down the road. The ornament could hang there all year unnoticed until the school janitor hacked it down with the hedge clippers and tossed it in the recycling bin. A little mouse. A little house. It was stupid, anyway.

She was still peering at the branch whose pin-sharp thorns would catch anything thrown in there when Aliya walked past. She was alone, and she was walking extra slow, wasn't she? Dragging her feet a little, wasn't she? Zoe gripped her handlebars and said her name, "Aliya," so quietly, it would be impossible for anyone to hear her, but Aliya turned around. Her brows tipped upward above her dark eyes. She didn't speak or step closer. But she didn't leave, either.

Zoe wanted to say, *I've missed you. Be my friend again. Don't go away.* But all she managed was a quiet, "Hey."

"Hey," said Aliya.

"Waiting for a ride?" asked Zoe.

"No. Walking home." Aliya turned to go. Zoe had to think of something else to say before she got away, but what? "Kind of wet out to walk that far." Stupid. Couldn't she think of something better to say than that?

"Nanni is sick, so I won't be getting a ride home today."

"Sick with what?"

"Sick with sadness," said Aliya. "And bad headaches."

"She misses her home in Pakistan."

Aliya's chin jutted out suddenly. "How did you know that?"

"You told me on Halloween. And she told me one time when she was making the *parathas*. Do you want to come over?"

Aliya stepped back, the invitation having been spat out about as delicately as a wad of gum. "What did you—"

"I'm asking you over," said Zoe. "To my house."

"To your house?"

"It's winter break," said Zoe. "Will you . . . come over?"

"Yes," said Aliya. Then came the smile, not the movie-cue grin she'd given Trish in the classroom, but the real one. "I've waited a long time for you to ask," she said.

Halfway home Zoe gave Aliya the ornament. Aliya held it up by the short, red string as they walked along. "A house and a mouse," she said.

"You can hang it on your Christmas tree."

"We don't celebrate Christmas."

Zoe steered her bike around a puddle. "Oh, right. I'm sorry."

"It's okay," said Aliya. "I'll hang it in my window."

"So you don't get to open presents? I mean, on Christmas morning?"

"We get money for toys and sweets when we celebrate Eid at the end of Ramadan."

"Oh, it can be an Eid present, then."

"Okay."

Zoe parked her bike in the carport and let them in with her key. The note on the kitchen table read:

Dear Zoe,
I'm at the gardening store. I'll be back soon. Hot cocoa and cookies for you and Juke. How about curry and chapatis for dinner?

Love,
Mom

Zoe made hot cocoa while Aliya called her mother. Later they fought with Juke over the last six chocolate-chip cookies. Then they danced around the kitchen with Merlin, his toenails going *clickity clack* on the kitchen floor. In Zoe's room they listened to Background Noise and talked about Jamal's new blue smile, courtesy of braces. The clouds blew westward, and the sun silvered the raindrops on Zoe's bedroom window.

"Look," said Aliya, pointing to a crack on the ceiling. "It's shaped like a bird."

"An owl, I think," said Zoe, nodding at the crack.

"Yeah." Aliya tilted her head to one side. "I can see that."

"Wanna see something else?"

"Sure."

They slipped on their coats and headed out back. Zoe nudged Mom's bag of potting soil aside and leaned against the storage shed to unlock the red door. She was about to let Aliya into her dreamroom, something she'd never done with Kellen back at home. But this dreamroom was bigger than her old closet at 18 Hawk Road. Maybe big enough for two.

She half listened to Aliya chatting behind her about the storage shed at her house, how it was crammed full of boxes now that all of Nanni's things had been shipped over from Pakistan. Her chatting stopped as soon as Zoe opened the door.

"Oh," she breathed out as they stepped inside.

Aliya scanned the drawings on the wall while Zoe shifted from foot to foot. She hadn't let anyone see her artwork since first grade. Aliya was standing very still now, almost too still.

"It's Julia," she said.

"It's from the photograph I saw on her cross," said Zoe.

"You left out the horse."

Zoe looked down. "I'm not ready to draw horses yet."

"You could take a sketch pad to Shepherd's Glen like Julia did."

"Yeah," said Zoe. She couldn't imagine doing that, but Julia's dad was taking riding lessons there for the first time. Maybe she could take a big step like that, learn to draw outside the way Julia had. Later, maybe later . . .

A gust of wind blew through the open door. Zoe closed it. Aliya turned back to the drawing of Julia. Zoe could hear her breath, going in, going out. "Are you afraid of dying?" she asked at last.

"Yeah," said Zoe. "Are you?"

Aliya nodded. "The Koran says that when we die, we go to a beautiful garden in which rivers flow."

"My grandma Nell talks about heaven like that, but my mom believes in reincarnation. She thinks we come back as something else."

"If I had to come back, I'd want to come back as a hawk," said Aliya.

"They have a huge wingspan," agreed Zoe.

Aliya spread her arms out wide. "It's like they float across the sky."

They sat down together on the big beanbag chair and looked out the window. A streak of sky unfurled a wide, blue ribbon above the trees.

"Why didn't you tell me you lived here at the trailer park? It doesn't matter what people like Mallory think. I would have come over months ago."

Zoe crossed her legs and poked her finger through the hole in her jeans. "It didn't have anything to do with Mallory or with the trailer park. It's . . . kind of a long story."

Aliya tilted her head and waited for more.

Zoe could have started the story anywhere. She might have started with the moment in her empty room when she'd slipped her Swiss army knife from her pocket and unscrewed her glass doorknob or with the big garage sale. But she began with hide-and-seek, the last game she'd ever played at 18 Hawk Road, and she told Aliya everything from the moment she first heard they'd lost their home forever to driving to Scout River and living in the van in secret for months above the graveyard. She even told Aliya about running away back home, hiding in the garage attic, the fire. Everything. And Aliya listened, with eyes wide and hands quiet in her lap. The story took a thousand years to tell, and it only took a half hour, and the sun was dipping down behind the trees when she was done.

They sat quietly together, the dreamroom filling with blue shadows until, at last, Aliya broke the silence.

"So now you're here with me," she said.

"Now I'm here with you."

"And you're home now?"

Zoe wrapped her arms around her knees. She didn't think she'd end up living in a mobile home on the banks of Scout River. But her family had a real address again. A front door and a back door. And just now she was here in her new dreamroom with Aliya, her drawings on the wall, her glass knob catching the last rays of sunlight the same way it had in her bedroom back in Tillerman.

"Find the door," Grandma had said. Crazy words that had echoed in her head all the way from California to Oregon, filling her eyes with dreams. She'd kept the glass knob and waited. Looking everywhere for the *one* door, the *right* door, to take her home.

But there were lots of doors in the world.

She knew that now and felt the knowing of it in her body.

Zoe stretched out her arms and leaned back in her beanbag chair.

"Yeah," she said. "I'm home."

Author's Note

You might say I wrote this story because my husband and I lived on the road for short periods of time when we were young and happy and foolish. You might say I wrote it because we moved fifteen times in the first sixteen years of our marriage, and our wandering lifestyle was hard on the kids. But the clue to the real reason I wrote this story is hidden at the bottom of my purse. It's a glass doorknob, like the one Zoe brings on her journey. I've been carrying it with me everywhere, since I began writing *The Double Life of Zoe Flynn* (not a smart thing to try to get through baggage check at the airport, I've discovered). The doorknob is a symbol for Zoe, and for me, because the home I left when I was thirteen had glass doorknobs. There's something magical about the house you grow up in. And the magic of my own childhood home draws me still. I dedicated this story to my sons, and to Martha Elke, but it's also for every child and every grown-up who has ever had to leave the home they loved behind. May you search far and wide for your place as Zoe did.

And may you find the door.